31/05/17

D1102556

## BRENT LIBRARIES

Please return/renew this item
by the last date shown.
Books may also be renewed by
phone or online.
Tel: 0115 929 3388
On-line www.brent.gov.uk/libraryservice

*Anson Goode*

9112000323873

Life Changing Books in conjunction with Power Play Books
Published by Life Changing Books
P.O. Box 423 Brandywine, MD 20613

This novel is a work of fiction. Any references to real people, events, establishments, or locales are intended only to give the fiction a sense of reality and authenticity. Other names, characters, and incidents occurring in the work are either a product of the author's imagination or are used fictitiously, as are those fictionalized events and incidents that involve real persons. Any character that happens to share the name of a person who is an acquaintance of the author, past or present, is purely coincidental and is in no way intended to be an actual account involving that person.

Library of Congress Cataloging-in-Publication Data;

www.lifcchangingbooks.net
13 Digit: 978-1934230497
10 Digit: 1934230499

# *Dedication* ...

This book is dedicated with love to everyone who is a part of the "Rainbow Coalition"

# Acknowledgments

I owe so many people so many thanks; I already know I'm not going to remember everyone so please charge it to my mind and not my heart. First I want to thank God for continuously blessing me with witty and creative ideas. It's in Him that I live, move and have my being. I want to thank my mom for always supporting me and giving that boost when I needed it. Toots, a lot of who I am is because of you. I love you, Daddy.

My children, Kenisha, Tarez'ia and Tarez, Azauriah, Jah'vyon and Ja' Lynn the reasons why I write. You all are my air. I couldn't breathe without you. Ain't no mountain, ain't no sea…to keep my sista away from me…I love you, Keesha… Infinitely. To my awesome publisher, Azarel, thank you for believing in my work and investing in me. You won't regret it. In a short time I have learned so much from you. As long as you are willing to teach, I am willing to learn. May God bless you 1000 times more than you already are.

Team Goode: Charonda T, what can I say? Here we go again, Sis…let's go harder…. Nikki S. This is our season, you are blessing to me and I appreciate you sooo much….Jaquita Bruner…..you have no clue how much your support truly means to me. Thank you for supporting my work and just being there for me. LaTasha Chappell…there is nothing I wouldn't do for you and I know the feelings are returned. Our sisterhood is one of a kind and I value it. LaTosha Quinn…I love you…you're my lil' sis…I haven't forgotten ....I got you…but I wanna thank you for keeping me "sucker free". Thank you for being there for me during one of the most trying times in my life. Regardless the circumstance, I am blessed that we met. To my friend Vanessa Mapp-Andell who is easily my biggest fan. Goode friends like you don't come along too often. I'm glad God sent you when He did. Kota Andrews for all of your creative input and kind words. And to all of my Interstate and Starwood friends and family you all make working a pleasure.

Kalia and Kiana Thomas…I just want you both to know that Laura would be so proud of the both of you…DO NOT LET ANYONE TELL YOU THAT YOU CAN'T DO IT!!

A huge thank you to my readers who make writing worthwhile. Writing means nothing if you have no one to read it. Thank you all so much. To my LCB family of authors- I thank you all for supporting this book and posting it all over. I got you!

There is a story in all of us dying to be told. The key is to tell it well. So to all of the aspiring authors out there my best advice to you is to keep on writing, reading and studying the publishing business. You can never know too much. And finally a very special thanks to C.S.B. because you left impressions on my soul as well.

****BE GOODE OR BE GOODE AT IT****
**AG**

# Prologue
........ ....

"You're one crazy bitch!" the woman shouted as she wiggled to break free from the ropes.

"Oh. So you wanna talk shit? Yeah, I'm deranged. Glad you noticed. I've known I was crazy for years. But I have someone who loves me now. As a matter of fact, the same person who claims to love you is the same person who loves me," the assailant stated, as anger filled his face.

"What the fuck are you talking about?"

"You are so fucking clueless. You must've been a blonde in your former life, dumb ass. I must admit, I'm quite jealous because our lover has never said to me what's been told to you in this bullshit ass note. Let's read it shall we?"

The note was immediately read with spite the entire time. There was a short pause before he found his voice after reading the letter, which was changing with every word spoken. "She would get you pregnant if she could, but since she can't, I'm sure that she would try to talk you into getting pregnant the old fashioned way, and the two of you raising that baby together. She has always wanted a baby. That's why you have to go because as much as I have to offer her, I can never give her that. I would never be able to compete with you, let alone win. And I hate losing. I won't lose," he finished morosely.

"What the hell is wrong with you? And why is your

voice changing? You gotta let me go, pleaseseeeeee," Morgan pleaded with her captor softly. "Please listen to me. My husband will give you whatever you want. I'm Morgan Calloway. He's worth millions. Just please let me go. I promise I won't go to the cops."

"Your man ain't paying shit and our boo is too busy licking the next bitch's pussy to worry about you."

"Stone loves me. She would never cheat on me. I don't know who you are or what this is but..."

Grabbing her arm tightly as Morgan fought to free herself from the chair, he spat! "But nothing, bitch. Her blood type is ho- negative. It's impossible for her to be faithful to anyone. Not me...you, not anyone. Now hold still. I got something for you. This won't hurt but it may sting slightly," he said, injecting the contents of the vials into Morgan's flinching arm. Morgan's eyes darted left to right as the poisons began to course through her veins.

"Let me go!" Morgan shouted! "I swear when I get out of here I'm going to fuck you up!"

"Such bravado. It won't do you any good. Soon enough the world will be minus one less skank."

Morgan tried to lift her arm but it felt like lead. She couldn't talk either. Slowly, tears ran down her face.

"Don't fight it. You can't win. It's Saxitoxin. In a few minutes, your whole body will be numb."

Morgan sat paralyzed. All she could do was watch the crazy person move about the room with purpose. The man had placed a sixty gallon steel drum on an induction heater that looked like a giant electric burner. He poured sodium hydroxide in the barrel and waited for it to heat. The temperature of the lye solution was three-hundred two degrees exactly. The young person smiled, thinking about the end result of the project. In a few hours the contents that would go into the barrel would be no more. All traces of evidence eradicated. No one would know what the drum once contained.

And Morgan's life...just like the others would end.

# Love Don't Live Here Anymore
● ● ● ● ● ● ● ● ● ● ● ● ● ● ● ● ● ● ● ● ● ● ● ● ● ● ● ● ● ● ● ● ● ● ● ●

"You're tuned into 101.5, W-H-O-T Radio, Atlanta's number one choice for hot grooves and smooth conversation. This is your favorite radio show, 'Symone Says' where anything and everything goes and I'm your host, Symone Morrow. Before I get out of here for the night, I just want to say congratulations to my wonderful fiancé, Keyon Steele, CEO of Man of Steele Records, for his phenomenal first five years in business. M.O.S. will be hosting a celebration bash that is second to none, and A-T-L, you all know from past experience when he throws a party he does it big."

"I'll keep you all posted on the date. I might even give away a prize to one of my loyal listeners to be my special guest at the star-studded event. So, until next time my peeps, remember to be good or be good at it."

Symone took her headset off and rubbed her temples. *What a night.* Although she loved her job, it seemed like the callers got crazier with each passing day; especially the woman who had been calling every other day for the past month. It had been funny at first, but now it was a bit disconcerting. When she answered the call, the caller always started screaming.

"You told my lover to leave me!" the caller said, crying.

"Hey, girl. I was wondering if you were going to call in or not. I was starting to miss you. Not! Why don't you say your name so I will finally know who I'm talking to?" Symone replied, laughing.

"It doesn't matter who I am. All that matters is that I know who you are. Watch your back, bitch!" The call ended abruptly.

"What kind of mess is this, Atlanta? You told Harpo to beat me?" Symone mocked, laughing at the woman after the caller hung up. *What a joke.*

Atlanta was full of quacks and that caller was one of them. Her show was not like Dr. Phil's. She didn't have any degrees in psychology or any licenses. She was just a regular person, talking with regular people, and listening to good music while she was at it. If they wanted to talk, she made it her job to listen. Only on the rare occasion that someone asked for her advice would she give it to him or her. But she hadn't told any man to leave his woman. The caller must have been mistaken. Symone just blew it off. She didn't take the caller seriously.

She threw some things in her tote bag and waved goodbye to her producer and co-workers. Before she left the floor, the security guard handed her a small package. She opened the box and saw that it contained Barbie doll, her head had been shaved, with a note attached that read, "*This could be you.*"

Shaking her head, she tossed the box in the trash. This was the third "gift" in three weeks. All nonsense. The thought to call the police hadn't crossed Symone's busy mind.

It was almost eleven at night and she was beat. By the time she made it home Keyon's car was in the driveway, which was not a huge surprise. Even with his late hours, it was rare that she beat him home.

She'd been spending a lot of time at the radio station working hard to develop new segment ideas for her show. It was rumored that her show was being considered for syndication. This was what she had worked so hard for all these years. She wanted her name to be synonymous with Michael Baisden, Tom Joyner and Rickey Smiley, who all had shows that were broadcasted nationally. In order for her to reach that goal, she knew that a few sacrifices would have to be made and time spent at home was one of them. As much as that should have bothered her, it didn't.

It was a sad fact, but life at home had changed drastically for the worst. She knew Keyon was avoiding being at home as much as possible, too. It was evident that things were different between them; Ray Charles could have seen that they needed help, but, both of them were too prideful to ask for it.

Demanding job schedules and lack of communication were eroding the foundation of their once solid relationship. Symone could think back to happier times between them. Times when everything was good, even the sex. Well, especially the sex. Come to think of it, they hadn't done that in over a month. She sat in the car in the driveway and allowed her mind to wander as she thought back to days long gone.

Keyon Steele was all that Symone had dreamed of when they first met. Not only was he tall, dark and handsome with a Morris Chestnut-like swagger and sex appeal, he was well on his way to becoming a self-made multi-millionaire. In truth, he looked like he could be Montell Jordan's twin, swagger and all. He had brains and brawn, and possessed a generous, loving spirit. He'd just formed Man of Steele Records when they met and worked very hard to make it a brand name. Her brother, Shymon and a few of his friends had formed a band and were trying to get a record deal. M.O.S. Records was looking for hot, unsigned artists so they hosted a talent showcase in Atlanta.

Most of the judges, who consisted of local radio personalities, and music executives, had counted out Shymon's group because all of them were so young and nerdy. The young men were between fifteen and seventeen years old. When they got on stage to sing, no one took them seriously. They bore a close resemblance to Steve Urkel, glasses, pocket protectors and all. All of the judges were talking amongst themselves when the host gave them their queue.

Then, Shymon belted out the lyrics to Tony Terry's *'When I'm With You'* and had all the little girls in the auditorium gasping and swooning, sliding down in their seats. Not only did the judges shut up and take notice, it brought Keyon from backstage to see who was singing. They blew everyone away, and the rest as they say, was history.

Symone had been checking Keyon out since they arrived. He was a magnificent sight to behold. And he had been checking her out, too. But as attractive as she found him, she would not make it easy for him.

After her brother's group had caught Keyon's attention, he did all that he could to try to talk with her. As her brother's legal guardian, Symone knew he was going to have to deal with her at some point. His stature made him appear intimidating so when he walked over to speak, she couldn't do anything but nod at first until she found her voice.

"Your brother and his friends are very talented. I believe they will have a promising recording career, and with the right guidance, longevity in the business." He spoke confidently.

"Yes, they are talented, but more than that, they are extremely intelligent."

"I see. Are you their manager? Should I have my people get with your people?" He tried lamely to crack a joke. Symone didn't laugh.

"What?" she said, sounding exasperated. "Look, whatever it is you're trying to do here is pointless. I'm not going to fuck you just so my brother can get a deal. So, all this bullshit ass, small talk you're spitting can stop. I do not do casual sex with anyone. No matter how rich or famous he *thinks* he is. And I, Sir, am not your typical woman nor am I a groupie. Here is our attorney's card. Her name is Sherry Sears. A name that I'm sure, even you have heard of. She will be expecting your call. Good day, Mr. Steele," she finished, and then stormed out of the building.

It was evident he'd never had anyone speak to him that way. Later on, Keyon told her that he wasn't trying to merely get her into bed, but he was genuinely interested in getting to know her better. It had frustrated him to no end that regardless of what he tried, she still didn't give him the time of day. She was challenging, and definitely not a groupie, and he was glad about that.

Symone was more wholesome than any woman he'd dated in the past. With her milk chocolate skin, big brown eyes, and pouty mouth, she looked like Keshia Knight-Pulliam, just taller. She was definitely the type of woman he could take home to meet his mother. But, no amount of calling, begging or pleading helped his cause.

Two months and a four-foot tall stuffed panda bear later, she finally conceded. Because of her reluctance to date him, he took things slowly, wining her and dining her, giving her the chance to get to know him better as well. They had gone out for six months before she felt she was ready to take their relationship to the next level.

That night, it was Keyon's intention to *only* cook dinner for her at his place and then take her home. But she had other plans. A week before the invitation, they'd been working out in his home gym together. After their workout they went to shower. Symone thought that he told her that she could take a shower in the hall bathroom, so she was shocked to find him there, naked in all his glory.

His limp dick hung about eight inches long, making her wonder how strong and long it could get when he was aroused. Her eyes never left his crotch. Symone just stood in the doorway, speechless, frozen in time, until water splashed on her chin. Mistakenly, she thought that he sprinkled water on her, but was embarrassed to realize she had been slobbering.

Once she regrouped she offered a mousey apology and left him to finish. She showered in his massive bedroom shower. After that, she couldn't close her eyes without seeing his nakedness in her mind. The desire to jump his bones was relentless. When he offered to cook for her at his home, she knew that would be the perfect time to make her move.

While he was in the kitchen, putting the finishing touches on dinner, she had excused herself to the restroom. When Symone got upstairs, she pulled a few things out of her large hand bag that she was going to need to make their first night together special, rose petals, condoms, and lubricant (just in case things got a little freaky).

Once she made it back downstairs, he was setting the table. Keyon prepared an exquisite dish of chicken and broccoli Alfredo, a tossed Caesar's salad, and lightly buttered bread sticks. For dessert, he had made a vanilla mousse cheesecake from scratch. He definitely knew his way around the kitchen. *Let's just hope it's the same for the bedroom* she thought to herself.

Never one to be considered a seductress, that tonight she was going to be. That night, she was not going to hold anything back from Keyon. At some point when she wasn't looking, she had fallen in love with him. She had shared her hurts and pains, hopes and dreams with him and now she was going to share her body with him.

At the end of their meal she had offered to help him clean up, but was grateful when he declined her help. She knew she didn't have much time to prepare. Upstairs, she made quick work of strategically sprinkling the rose petals on the floor in the bed. She grabbed the CD out of her purse full of her old school slow jams, the ones she listened to often. Putting it into the stereo, she set the volume low, but loud enough to help set the mood. Then she undressed at lightning speed almost falling over the edge of the bed when her foot got caught in the hem of her jeans. She raced to the bathroom and brushed her teeth and took what her grandmother used to call a 'ho bath', a wash off in the sink. Now that she was fresh and clean she put on her lingerie.

The stage was set.

He was the only thing missing. When he called for her, and she didn't answer, he came upstairs to see what was keeping her. When he opened the door to his bedroom he was delighted at the scene that played out before him.

Jodeci was playing on the stereo when he stepped inside. *Come and talk to me, I really wanna meet you. Can I talk to you? I really wanna know you.*

He continued to hum along with the soulful crooners as he walked further into the room. Symone strutted out of the bathroom wearing a sheer red mesh baby doll negligee'. He knew it had come from Victoria's Secret because he'd picked it out in hopes that one day he would see her in it. Her thick thighs and long legs glistened. The perfume that she wore permeated the air as she drew closer to him.

She pulled out all the stops for him. Shaky fingers unbuttoned his shirt when she reached him. His lips parted in an effort to speak but she put her index finger to his mouth and said, "Sshhh, no words. Not tonight."

She removed his leather loafers and socks, massaging his feet after doing so. Next, she unfastened his belt and pants, removing them and his boxers in one fell swoop. Boys II Men's '*Uh-Ah*' began to play. Symone positioned her man in the middle of his California king-sized bed and sat him down. He watched her intently as she slowly peeled the sexy lingerie from her body. D-cup breasts sprang free. She sucked her two index fingers to wet them and used them to play with her nipples.

"You like this baby?" she asked seductively.

He nodded his head. "Yes."

"Good," Symone replied before kneeling in front of him and taking his dick into her mouth. Up and down in slow motion she sucked. She drenched his dick with her peppermint-flavored saliva. Symone lifted his hard tool and licked his swollen balls, savoring each one like a delicacy. With her right hand she held the base of his engorged shaft while using her left hand to play in her own wetness. Her jaws gripped him tight like a pair of vice grip's. His hands grabbed her head as he began to pummel her face with his dick.

"Ah shit, Symone! I love the way you suck my dick. This shit is amazing. Where- you-learn-this-shit-at-ba-by?" he said in agonizing pleasure through each thrust. She fingered herself and moaned loudly as juices dripping down her thighs. She was about to cum.

"Oh shit, Keyon," she managed between sucks. They exploded at the same time. She came in her own hand and he came in her mouth.

Letting him rest a paltry five minutes, Symone slowly licked him back to his long, luscious and thick ten inches and climbed on for the ride of her life. She parted her nether lips with two fingers and slid only the tip of his dick in before pulling up, repeating the action several times but each time going down further until Keyon couldn't take it anymore. The next time she took him in her he grabbed her by the waist and impaled his dick inside.

Symone cried out his name, shocked by the size of him. They found a rhythm and began to make music with their bodies. She gyrated on his dick and threw the pussy at him. Keyon caught it with pleasure. He leaned forward as she rode him and he sucked her breasts, giving each one equal amounts of attention. Her nipples were hard enough to cut diamonds.

With each flick of his tongue, she felt tiny pulses of electricity course through her body. His hands cupped her ass cheeks and he rolled them over, his dick only slipping out of the wet pocket briefly. He commenced a steady glide, massaging her insides and hitting every G spot he knew she had, using creative strokes to find new ones. The couple kissed, fondled and loved on one another until they were both spent.

In the aftermath, Keyon had snaked his arm under Symone's side, pulling her close to him so they could spoon.

"I love you so much, baby."

"I love you, too."

But that was then.

Now, she and Keyon could barely be in the same room with one another without arguing. And arguing seemed to be the only time they spoke. Symone grabbed the bag next to her and exited the car, dreading going inside. Little did Symone know there was someone watching, lurking in the shadows; and a black town car with a license plate that read BLUD-MNY sitting close by.

# Cheating In The Next Room

On the West End, Donita "Donnie" Stone was enjoying her latest conquest, tasting her sweet delights. Strawberries and cream, Patron and pussy were on the menu. The creamy texture of the whipped cream mixed and mingled with her current lover's pussy juices, stimulating her palate. Monique? Misha? Or was it Mona? Either way, she was fine as hell.

Donnie couldn't remember her name nor did she give a fuck. She just called her 'Boo'. All she knew was that when she saw her at Club Exotica, she wanted her big juicy ass in her face for the rest of the night. What's-her-name's waist was tiny as hell and her ass looked like she was holding two basketballs in her pants. Her low-cut jeans revealed her perfect heart-shaped ass. Before the night was over, Donnie knew she had to hit that.

After a few drinks and a little conversation, Donnie had her exactly where she wanted her, spread eagle in her bed. Donnie's wet tongue slid over Boo's pearl tongue and circled it. She inserted her stiff tongue inside her pussy, thoroughly licking her walls, trying to get as deep as she could. Her face was so far in the girl's pussy; her nose was rubbing her clit, creating even more excitement. Donnie continued to explore the pink cavern with her tongue and fingers, sliding them in and out, fucking her until her legs shook and she was on the verge of a volcanic eruption. Donnie replaced her tongue with her prosthetic dick as she climbed inside the wet cave. As the almost life-like strap-on penetrated Boo, Donnie applied pressure to her clitoris with her fingers, caressing it.

"Damn, Donnie. You loving' me so good. Fuck this pussy baby. Please don't stop."

Donnie had no intention of stopping, not anytime soon anyway. Although it was Boo's body Donnie was making love to, it was another woman's face she was seeing. The picture in her head was of the woman she knew she just had to have. It made Donnie's own pussy gush just thinking about her. Thoughts of the other woman's beautiful body and sexy demeanor made Donnie increase her rhythm.

For the next hour she pounded and fingered Boo's pussy, causing her to whimper with both pain and pleasure. The friction burned the two women lovers up. Boo wrapped her legs around Donnie's waist and used both of her hands to push Donnie as deep as she could inside of her. With the force of a runaway train, they both came. Happy to have found release but still not satisfied, Donnie got up to shower, inviting Boo to come with her. This was the best way to get her guest out of her house without being rude. If the pussy was good, and Boo's was, she might want to call the chick back over. She couldn't burn any bridges.

When they showered and dressed, the couple went to breakfast at the IHOP near the mall right around the corner from Boo's house.

"Yo, lemme get them digits from you again. Here, put your info in my phone," Donnie asked, handing her the cell phone after they had finished eating.

This way she could get the girl's name without having to admit that she forgot it in the first place. The girl obliged and gave Donnie her phone back, thanking her for a wonderful night and expressing interest in seeing her again soon, as Donnie walked her back to her car. Donnie looked at the phone when she got in her own car and smiled as she drove off. The girl's name was Sasha.

• • • • • • • • • • • • • • • • •

Charmaine Franklin, Donnie's on-again-off-again girl-friend, rewound the footage she'd just taped. The more she watched it, the angrier she got. Her breathing became shallow, and her heart was beating so hard she could hear the quick, hard beats pounding through her chest. Hell, it was so loud the neighbors could probably hear it, too. She stomped down from her bedroom in the attic of Donnie, and her brother, Damian's home.

"Donnie is so fucking disrespectful!" she exclaimed, talking to herself out loud. "How is she gonna bring another bitch into our home? Into our bed? She got me so fucked up!" Charmaine yelled, pounding her right fist into her left hand.

"Always trying to play me for a fool and then when I ask her if she is fucking around on me, what does that lying bitch say? *No, Charmaine. I would never do you like that, Charmaine. I love you, Charmaine.* Love me my ass. If this shit is love then that bitch can keep it! I'm not taking any more of her shit. Ugh!"

Charmaine stormed around the house after she emptied and rinsed out her makeshift toilet, which was nothing more than a tin mop bucket, and then she fixed herself something to eat. Damian was out of town so she didn't have to worry about him coming home anytime soon and she knew Donnie was headed to work after her sexcapade with ol' girl. Charmaine knew Donnie so well that she figured she was calling the woman 'Boo' because she didn't know her whole name. *Just like Donnie to fuck a stranger. Ho ass!* All of her infidelities were taking their toll on Charmaine and the shit was about to hit the fan.

It was Donnie's constant lying about being faithful that made Charmaine decide to wire her house with surveillance equipment in the first place. Even though her gut told her that Donnie was cheating she never did have any solid proof. Now, she had irrefutable evidence. Donnie just couldn't be trusted. Her doggish ways ignited many heated arguments in the past, leading to too many fistfights.

Charmaine had showed up at Grady Memorial Hospital far too many times to have her blackened, cut eye, stitched or her bruised ribs bandaged. The night that Donnie had called into the radio show 'Symone Says', the two of them had just fought. Donnie had told the host that her girlfriend was crazy. The host, who clearly thought that Donnie was a dude because she kept referring to her as 'sir', told her that no one deserved to be in an abusive relationship, man or woman, and for "him" to end things before things got out of hand.

Charmaine had it in for the host ever since. Donnie's calling into that show had hurt worse than Charmaine cared to admit. After the fight, she was escorted to a domestic violence shelter and Donnie was carted off to jail. Unfortunately, Donnie's brother paid her bond and she was released a few hours later. But while she was in the shelter she'd decided to stop getting mad and start getting even. Charmaine did love Donnie and wanted things to work between them. She just wanted Donnie to stop hitting, lying and cheating on her. But that wasn't going to happen. No matter how good Charmaine tried to be, no matter how much she tried to love Donnie, it was evident that she was not going to change. Donnie thought Charmaine was stupid and that she could do any and every thing to her without recourse. Now, her lying ex-girlfriend and that meddling host were on her shit list. The last place anyone wanted to be.

Charmaine walked around checking all the cameras and microphones that she strategically placed around the house a few weeks ago. Once all the equipment was checked and the kitchen cleaned, Charmaine took her pail back to the attic and grabbed the laptop she used to monitor the house. She had a few errands to run before paying a visit to Ms. Sasha. It had rained overnight making it even more humid than it already was in Atlanta. The heat almost took her breath away when she stepped out onto the porch. She walked the two blocks to Mosley Park where she parked her car, got in and drove away. Traffic had begun to let up as she merged onto I-20 East. It wouldn't take her long to handle her business. Not long at all.

• • • • • • • • • • • • • • • • • •

Sasha Jones hated waiting for the cable company. Every time she called and needed them to come out they could never give her a set appointment. They seemed to take pleasure in taking up her whole day and spreading the time in three-hour blocks.

*"We can send a technician out between nine and twelve noon, one to four or five to eight. Which will be better?"* the customer service representative asked.

None of them would really work, but she chose the one to four p.m. time slot. After the two nights she spent with Donnie she needed the extra hours sleep. She always left her spent and exhausted.

She was getting her hair flat-ironed at five-thirty for a video shoot and couldn't be late. She'd told Donnie before she left her house that she needed to get home to wash her hair and deep condition it before her appointment. Donnie liked running her fingers through her hair and was happy that Sasha didn't have any tracks in it. Hell, Sasha loved the fact that Donnie was digging her. She'd even given her a pet name already, Boo. Normally Sasha didn't like such terms of endearment but with Donnie it was just...different.

A short white, chubby guy rang her doorbell and Sasha thanked the powers that be that it was the cable guy. He'd showed up exactly at one o'clock.

"Yeah, I'm Larry. I came to look at your equipment," the man said.

"Right this way. It's the box in my bedroom. Normally, all they have to do is send a signal to the box to get it to work but this time it didn't work. I guess I need a new one."

"Well, that's what I'm here to check for you, Miss. I'll get right on it."

"Thanks. I'll be in the living room making a few calls. Holler if you need me."

With that, she left the room and let the man do his work. He changed out her box in less than five minutes and called in to the customer service department to report the box had been installed and for them to send a signal to ensure it was operating correctly.

Minutes later, he packed up his tools and then stepped into her bathroom, looking around. On the counter was a jar of Queen Rayvene's deep penetrating conditioner. That was some smelly shit, but it did make women's hair silky and smooth. He emptied the contents of the jar and rinsed it down the sink then reached in his bag and pulled out a bottle of his own. He filled the conditioner jar with the new substance, recapped the jar and put it back on the sink.

"I'm done here lil' lady. Er'thing's all set."

"Thank you so much. Have a great day."

"You too. Good day."

Sasha jumped in the shower; washed and rinsed her hair, and applied an ample amount of leave-in conditioner to it. She put a plastic cap over her head before heading towards her hair dryer. She set the timer for fifteen minutes. Once the conditioner started to warm she noticed that the smell was different from before but didn't pay much attention to it. The dryer bell chimed as usual and she went to rinse her hair in the kitchen sink. The warm water felt good to her head.

"What the fuck is going on?" Sasha yelled as she watched her hair fall out in clumps and rinse down the sink. Tears started flowing down her face as fast as her hair ran down the drain.

"Oh God, what is this? Why is this happening?"

When Sasha turned the faucet off and ran to the mirror she screamed in complete horror. All her hair was gone. She was as bald as a newborn baby.

Not understanding what could have gone wrong, she ran and picked the conditioner jar out of the trashcan. She scraped the side of the jar and took a little cream out and put a little on a small patch of her arm. It looked like her conditioner but it smelled differently. She rinsed the spot where the 'conditioner' had been and in less than three minutes the hair on her arm was gone. Her conditioner wasn't conditioner after all. It was Nair. There was a piece of paper on the bottom with a note written on it, "Fuck with Donnie again and your hair won't be the only thing you lose."

• • • • • • • • • • • • • • • • •

"Are you sure I not get any trouble, Larry? I new here and need this job." the Hispanic technician asked in broken English.

"I'm sure, Paco. It's all taken care of. I'm just glad I caught you when I did. Here's a lil' something for your help," Larry said. He handed the technician five crisp one hundred dollar bills, then watched him drive off. It wasn't until Larry was back in his home did he relax. He took off his jumpsuit, wig, and prosthetic facemask and washed the day's job away, revealing his true self.

Lying across her bed, Charmaine smiled. She was pleased with how she'd pretended to be a cable technician. And when she was happy she sang. "Sa-sha's hair was falling out; falling out, falling out; Sa-sha's hair was falling out, my bald lady."

# The Right Place At The Right Time

The day had begun fucked up for Symone and had gotten progressively worse. She looked stunning in her off-white, sleeveless, Roberto Cavalli dress. Diamonds were draped across her neck and adorned her wrists and fingers. This was her night.

In a few moments, she was going to receive the coveted Sister of the Year award from My Sister's Keeper, an organization that focused on helping at-risk girls from impoverished or lower-income families. But presently, she stood next to her car on 285 West, two miles down from her exit, pissed off, while the AAA service technician changed her flat tire.

By the time she arrived, the W Hotel Perimeter was packed with guests in their formal attire. She looked around the room at her co-workers and colleagues and offered them the fakest smile she could muster up. Although this was a night that she should have been genuinely happy, she wasn't. Only six out of the eight people she had invited even bothered to show up on time. One person was on the way, but the other? Well, she had no clue where he was. Keyon was missing in action.

Embarrassed, she told her friends and family that Keyon had an emergency at his company. In truth, she had no idea where he was or what was keeping him from being with her. She even had Judy, his assistant, put the event on his calendar so that he wouldn't forget and no matter what his reason was, she wasn't going to forgive him for a long time. She hadn't asked him for anything in a while. She at least wanted him here with her to help celebrate this honor. Tonight was not the night to pull this kind of stunt. She exhaled slowly and attempted to sound light as she joined the conversation with the others.

● ● ● ● ● ● ● ● ● ● ● ● ● ● ● ● ●

"Hey, there young fella," the older waiter said across the room, touching the young man on his shoulder. "Will you please go make sure that our guests' drinks are fresh? Start at the front and work your way back."

"Sure thing," Donnie said, pushing the beverage cart.

It always made her laugh when people mistook her for a dude. The old man, Walt, had been calling her 'young fella' since she'd gotten to the hotel. She'd been working a series of temporary jobs for the past few weeks in an attempt to stack her chips. At first, she didn't want to take it but now, she was glad that she did. Who would've guessed that she would be serving at the very banquet Symone Morrow was attending? The Gods were smiling down on her.

Before Walt had spoken to her, she was busy admiring the woman from across the room. Being the self-appointed expert on women's emotions as she claimed to be, she got the feeling that Symone was not as happy as she should have been. Not happy enough for a woman who was receiving a prestigious award, anyway. One thing Donnie noticed was that her fiancé was not there. *Trouble on the home front, I hope.* Donnie thought as she tended to the guests speedily. When she got to Symone's table, she made sure to linger. When she reached for Symone's glass, their fingers brushed for a brief second. Electricity shot through Donnie's arms causing her to spill a few droplets of water on the tablecloth near Symone's phone.

"Pardon me, ma'am. I didn't get any water on your phone, did I?" Donnie asked apologetically.

"No. You're fine," Symone said clearly, then mumbled, "it's not like he's going to call me anyway."

"Excuse me?" Donnie asked. But she heard exactly what she said. *When opportunity knocks, I will damn sure open the door.*

"Nothing. Will you guys excuse me? I'm going to go outside for a breath of fresh air. I will be back before they serve dinner."

Symone got up from the table and made her way outside. Donnie quickly refreshed the drinks and told her co-worker she was going out for a smoke. When she got outside she saw that Symone was on the phone with someone so she stood out of sight, yet close enough to hear.

"It doesn't matter what his excuse is. This is the second time he has done me like this on a night that was special to *me*. Hell, it's not like I have that many to count. It's not like I'm him or even my brother now for that matter. The two of them have people clamoring to give them shit all day and night." Donnie heard her say.

"What-the-fuck-ever. You're supposed to be my fucking friend but every time Keyon and I have an issue, it seems that you and Devine are always taking his side. I need to find me a friend who only knows me and not him, too. For once, I just want someone on my side, Jynx." Donnie watched Symone pace back and forth as she listened intently to the person on the other end.

"Yeah, I know it, girl. You are my best friend and I love you, too. Just make sure you hurry up and bring your slow ass on. Dinner is about to be served. Yes, I'm still coming to Piedmont Park Sunday. Okay, well, we can talk about that later. Don't break any more traffic laws than you already have. I will see you in a sec."

Symone pressed the end button on her cell phone oblivious to the fact that she wasn't alone. Donnie stood there in awe, happy that she had the chance to get this close to her; even more ecstatic that she was able to find out more about what was going on with her and her man. *If she is going to be in Piedmont Park on Sunday, so will I.* Symone took a deep breath and turned to go back into the hotel while Donnie still lurked in the shadows of the night.

Not too long after she was seated at the table did her best friend, Jynx, come sauntering in. She was a breathtakingly beautiful woman and there wasn't a man alive who didn't try to get with her, with the exception of Keyon, only because he was her first cousin.

He'd always made Symone feel as if *she* were the most beautiful woman on the planet, but lately, his attention had been diverted elsewhere. This is why Symone thought that he was cheating on her. Her friends refused to believe that he was capable of that. But anyone could cheat. Of that, she was sure.

Not willing to spend any more time focusing on who was not there, she decided to enjoy the rest of her evening with the people who cared enough to show up. After they ate cardboard tasting steak that was served, the awards ceremony was under way. The host presented each recipient with his or her award, saving the Sister of the Year award for last. Symone knew that hers would be the last presentation of the evening and she was hoping that Keyon would show up to see her receive her award and make her speech, but he never did. They ended the ceremony and everyone prepared to go their separate ways.

"Are you sure you don't want me to go home with you, Sweet-tart?" Devine asked Symone.

"No babe, I'm good. Don't you have a date tonight anyway?"

"Girl, you know I do. Naughty Devine will be showing her ass in more ways than one tonight." The three friends laughed. Devine, whose real name was Devrin Miller, was Symone and Jynx's flamboyantly homosexual best friend who kept them looking great and laughing. He turned into Naughty Devine after hours and although he didn't dress in full drag garb, he did beat his face and could work a pair of Christian Louboutin heels better than any woman they knew.

"Look, both of you bitches need to get out of here and have a great Friday night. We can get up this weekend for brunch as usual, okay?" Symone said.

"Okay," they agreed in unison and left as soon as the

valet brought their cars around.

Symone stood alone for a brief moment until her car arrived. Donnie watched her get into her car and made a mental note of the license plate -TALK2ME- as the other woman drove away.

Tears streamed down Symone's face as she drove down the Georgia 400 towards home. She turned on the radio and almost laughed at the Snoop Dogg track that bumped through her car speakers. *If bitches ain't shit but hoes and tricks, what did that make dudes? Pussies and punks,* Symone surmised. She glanced over at the lead crystal award that sat in the passenger seat and thought about her missing mate. What was so important to Keyon that he would miss her big night? It had to be something so serious that he couldn't get out of, right? A dull ache began to pound in her head then slowly made its way to her chest. She was heartbroken and hurt.

There were no lights on in the house when she pulled up. Only the exterior light came on over the garage when she pulled into the driveway. Imagine her surprise when the garage door opened and she saw none other than Keyon's Jaguar Super Sport parked in its usual spot. From the paint to the interior and the rims, the car was customized and had cost Keyon an arm and a leg. He loved that car, which made Symone want to buss the windows out of his car. Instead of following her heart and destroying his property, she chilled. Atlanta police would have no problem carting her off to jail if Keyon got them involved.

Symone waltzed in angrily. The moment she heard music playing loudly in Keyon's studio, her fury grew. "Keyon!" she shouted. "Keyon!"

The music was so loud, Symone couldn't even hear herself think, so she knew he didn't hear his name being called. Symone threw her keys on the kitchen counter and made her way to the studio. When she opened the door, her eyes flew immediately to the mirror that encompassed the entire far wall. All she could see was Keyon's huge office chair and a woman grinding up and down. The girl was making fuck faces. Evidently he was giving it to her right.

"Ain't this a bitch?" Symone yelled. Her arm was heavy and she realized she still had the award in her hand. She lifted her arm and threw it at the mirror, shattering it into thousands of tiny pieces. The terrified couple hit the floor and she went over to the sound system and powered it off.

"You mean to tell me that your ass stayed home to fuck some bitch in our home, *our home,* Keyon, instead of coming to support me? I can't believe this shit! Is this the reason you can't give me the dick, because you're giving it to someone else? Son-of-a-bitch! My black ass is going to jail tonight!" She lunged for the chair.

"Hold up there, Ma. Calm down. What the hell are you doing?" The young man said crawling away from her with his pants down to his ankles.

"Who the fuck are you?" Symone yelled, half confused and half happy that the stranger wasn't Keyon. "This is my damn house. How in the hell did you get in here? And where the fuck is Keyon?"

"I'm Ransom, Shymon's friend. I think Keyon is upstairs in his room," the frightened young man said.

"Why are you fucking in my house? This ain't a damn brothel. I can't believe this shit. Eww!" Symone stormed off. The young couple scurried to grab their clothes and offered their meager apologies before taking a seat in the living area.

"Shymon, get your fucking ass down here! I can't believe you would allow someone to fuck in my house. And you nor Keyon brought your punk asses to my big ni-"

"Sshhh. Will you shut the fuck up?" Shymon interrupted quietly. "Keyon is trying to rest."

"What do you mean he's trying to rest? He needs to get down here."

"He's hurt," Shymon nodded.

"What happened to him, Shymon?" Symone questioned with a worried look on her face.

"I don't know what exactly happened, but I'm guessing

he was in some sort of accident. All I know is he looks fucked up. I got dropped off this afternoon so we could go to the tailor and found him in the garage in bad shape. I took him to the hospital and they said he has bruised ribs. He wasn't even worried about himself. All he kept talking about was not wanting to miss your big night. They gave him some meds to put him out."

"What! I better go and check on him. Oh, by the way," Symone said, turning to face her brother, "the next time you let your lil' friends fuck in my house, I'm kicking your ass and theirs too. Get it?"

"Got it."

"Good. Now go home. I got it from here."

"I didn't drive, should I take Keyon's Aston Martin since the Jag is fucked up?"

"Nice try. My keys are on the kitchen counter. Take my Range."

"You got some gas in that joint? I may wanna hit up some hot spots."

"Shymon, don't you have any money? You are the only person I know who has hit records, won not one, but two Grammy's, and yet you *never* have any money," she finished, handing him a C-note.

"I do have money, but I still like getting it from you."

"Go, boy!" Symone said, swinging playfully in his direction. "Make sure you turn off the lights and set the alarm before you leave, please."

"Gotcha. Love you, Sis."

"Love you, too."

The room was dark with the exception of the low light from the television. Keyon lay sprawled across the bed with the cover draped across his waist. His bare chest and legs were exposed, his ribs bandaged. Symone immediately began to worry as she pulled the comforter over him. She sat in the chair next to the bed and watched him sleep. She couldn't believe that she thought he was callous enough to bring another woman into their home. What was wrong with her? *I can't believe I de-*

*stroyed the mirror in his studio. He is going to kick my ass when he sees that. What am I going to tell him?*

As time passed, Symone began to feel drained. She got out the chair and lay in the bed next to Keyon and drifted off to sleep. By the time she woke up, Keyon had already gotten the 4-1-1 from Shymon about her tantrum, and had cleaned most of the glass up in his studio. She crept around the corner with a guilty look on her face when she heard the glass tinkling as it hit the dustpan.

"Baby, what happened to you?" she asked concerned.

"I had a little accident. I'm good, though," he said, bending slowly to get the last of the glass.

"What kind of accident? And with you? Was it your fault?"

"Symone, what's with all the questions?"

"Because you're my man, and you're wrapped in bandages around your waist, barely able to stand up straight. I need to know what happened."

"Look, I'll explain later. But what's with you thinking I was fucking another woman?"

Symone simply folded her arms and pressed her body against the wall. Her defeated expression said it all.

Keyon allowed his eyes to roam her thick hips and curvaceous body. "I already spoke to your brother and I know he ain't lying. You are my fiancé, Symone. If I wasn't ready to be your husband, I never would've asked you to marry me. I'm not a cheater. I never have been and I don't plan on starting now. As much as you and I have been through, I can't believe that you don't trust me."

"I do trust you, babe," she offered quietly.

"You fucking threw your award through a plate glass mirror. And you scared the hell outta your brother's friends. I missed one night that was important to you and now you think that I don't give a fuck about what you have going on?"

"You can't say that my suspicions are unfounded. Something bad just happened to you and you don't wanna talk about it. You shut me out of everything important in your life and you spend so much time at work," Symone's fingers curled into air quotes, "that we never have sex and we can't stand to be in the same room with one another anymore."

"That's because it ain't shit to talk about. Damn! And just because I own M.O.S. doesn't mean that I don't have a job to do. I've been working my ass off to make sure that you, my family and my staff are taken care of. I'm not cheating on you. If you don't believe I spend all that time at work all you have to do is come to my office and find out."

Shaking his head, he continued, "You're unbelievable, you know that? You sit up and talk all this shit on your radio show about loving and trusting your mate, but that's all it is. Talk. Talk is cheap Symone, and I am all talked out. For the record, I love being in the same room with you. Glad to know how *you* really feel, though. Congratulations, by the way."

With a disgusted look he dumped the last of the glass in the garbage pail and walked out of the room, clearly still in pain. Symone heard the automatic garage door open and the soft purr of Keyon's engine starting. Then the only thing that she heard was the sound of her own sobs and the crack ripping through her breaking heart.

• • • • • • • • • • • • • • • • •

The weed and feed store in Jasper, Georgia was packed. It was almost seedtime and harvest and everyone was stocking up on their fertilizers and supplies. Charmaine had about six large bags of fertilizer herself and was busy looking at her list to make sure she had everything she needed.

> ~~6 large bags of fertilizer~~
> ~~Commercial bleach~~
> ~~12 metal pipes w/ screw caps~~
> ~~Twine~~
> ~~Cement~~
> ~~Boning knife~~
> ~~Electrical or duct tape~~

~~*1000 matches*~~
*Can of tennis balls*
*Mini-zip lock bags*
*Cornish hens*

"You got everything you need there, Marsha?" the store clerk asked.

"I sure do, Hank. You always take such good care o' me when I come in."

"Well, what else can I do for a perty lil' thing like you? You just make sure you don't stay away so long next time."

"Now, don't you fret your head 'bout that. I'll be moving back to the ranch for a lil' while so I can get me some R &R. That city is darn near driving me crazy."

"It sure will be nice to see you more often. Mebbe you and I can go to the church social together if you're back in time."

"Why, Hank, that'd be awful lovely. Awful lovely indeed. I'll see you soon, handsome."

"You come back now, ya hear?"

Charmaine waited for the bagger to load her things in her truck and she waved good-bye to her neighbors. One stop to the local grocer and she would be able to get the last things on her list. She loved it when a plan came together and that made her happy.

"Come and listen to a story 'bout a girl named Don, fuck so many bitches thought she had it going on, but then one day she met a girl named, Char, and tried to play her stupid but she took it to far..games that is, Monopoly...Now all the bitches Donnie fuck are gonna end up hurt, Char is taking names and then she's putting in work, they shoulda listened when she warned'em to stay outta Donnie's bed, 'cause now these fucking bitches 'gon end up dead.

# When Fate Has Her Way

Symone, Jynx, and Devine sat at the Flying Biscuit enjoying their breakfast and weekly catch-up sessions. Every Sunday it was breakfast first and then they walked across the street to Piedmont Park. Today would be different because Jynx had something to do for Keyon's anniversary party and Devine was too tired to do any walking after the date he had last night.

"You know you two are wrong for leaving me hanging like this," Symone said.

"No, bitch, we would have been wrong if we didn't show up at all. Your ass is lucky we even came to breakfast. What your ass needs is a life," Devine retorted.

"I have a life, thank you very much. I just happen to love spending time with my two Bff's that's all. Apparently neither of you can say the same."

"Well, Keyon asked me to handle a few things for him for his party that's coming up in a few weeks and I told him that I would. I still don't understand why he would ask me to help him and not you. You *are* his woman after all," Jynx mentioned.

"And you are his cousin, which means you can easily do it, too. Plus, you know he is still mad at me about the other day. Hell, he's really mad now because the estimate to get that mirror replaced is over eight grand, and you know how his ass hates spending money unnecessarily. You would think he was on the verge of becoming a pauper, he's so cheap."

"He's not cheap, Sweetart, he's parsimonious," Devine

offered with a laugh.

"You and those damned words. Call it what you will, but at the end of the day, it all means the same thing," Jynx added. "And we all know how frugal, cheap, penny-pinching or even *parsimonious* Keyon can be." The group broke out laughing.

"Seriously though, Symone," Devine began, "what are you going to do to get things back on track between you and Keyon? You can't just leave things as they are."

"I really didn't do anything wrong other than break that damn glass and I will offer to pay for the damage. But let's keep it real, if he were handling his business with me then I never would have flown off the handle like that in the first place."

"Wow, girl. I never thought I would say this, but you and Keyon could really benefit from one of my counseling sessions," Jynx commented.

"He can, but I'm good. I told him that I was sorry and that I trusted him. What more does he want from me?"

"Try honesty for once. You couldn't possibly trust him if you thought he was in that studio fucking some other woman. For the past seven or eight weeks we have been coming to this same restaurant, sitting at the same table, listening to the same story. '*I think Keyon is cheating on me. Keyon doesn't love my anymore. Things are different at home.*' Devine and I have been giving you the same advice, which is talk to him. But you haven't done that, have you?"

"I tried talking to him and it didn't work. I know something is going on with him but he keeps shutting me out."

"No, what you did was yell, not talk. You have to use *I* statements that take responsibility for your feelings, thoughts and behavior's. *You* statements come across as blaming or judgmental. Symone, you have to find a kinder way to say things," Jynx finished.

"Okay, okay, Dr. Jacobi. This is *not* one of your counseling sessions and I am *not* one of your patients," Symone quipped. She wasn't angry at her friend's assessment because she knew her advice was coming from a good place.

"I'm a marriage, family and sex therapist with clients, not patients. And I can't tell. Hell, every time we get together it's always The Symone Show. If Devine or I had something going on you would never know because you never shut up about your damned self long enough to find out about the others around you."

"Okay!" Devine said, snapping twice in the air. "You obviously have something on your mind, so honey chile you can have the floor."

"Well, since you both insist," she said and they all laughed. "There is this guy who works over at Man of Steele Records that I like."

"Get outta here! And you're just now saying something about it?" Symone said.

"Well, his name is Jon and he is in charge of marketing and public relations. A few weeks ago, Keyon and I went out to lunch, and I met him when I was at the office. He is very, very sexy."

"I didn't know you had lunch with Keyon, Jynx. When did this happen?" Symone questioned, cutting her eyes at her friend.

"It was July 9th. Three weeks ago. Anyway, Keyon asked him if he wanted to come out with u…"

"Why didn't you tell me you were having lunch with him? He didn't even mention it to me," Symone interrupted rudely.

"What are you saying, Symone? I don't like what you're implying. Do you think that Keyon and I are kissing cousins, is that it? 'Cause I can assure you that nothing is going down."

"I don't think that. But it's awfully funny that everyone is making dates with my man and I'm the one left out in the cold. You just up and have lunch with him out of the blue and shit."

"You need to check yourself, for real, Symone. This is getting out of hand."

"What? It had to be something special because you remembered the exact date and everything," Symone said accusingly.

"Are you fucking kidding me?"

"Girl, quit playing," Devine said. "Symone, you and I both know she had a lunch date with him."

"Whatever. I don't care. But why was it so important that she would need to remember every single detail?" Symone's eyes narrowed when she looked at Jynx. "July 9th, indeed. What's so fucking special about that?"

"July 9th is Keyon's birthday, Symone. Please don't tell me you forgot?" Devine asked sadly. The astonished look on her face told him that she had. Her mouth was open and she closed it fast and covered it with her hand. Tears formed in her eyes, threatening to spill over.

"Well, hell. That explains it," Jynx added throwing her hands in the air.

"Explains what?" Symone asked softly.

"You didn't get me anything for my birthday this year either. If you forgot his birthday it's only natural you would forget mine also, since we were born on the same date."

"Oh my gosh. Jynx, please forgive me. I have been so wrapped up in the new programming at the station and my mind has been in La-La Land. There have been talks about my show going into syndication and that's huge. Girl, I am so-o-o-o sorry. Can you please forgive me? For everything?"

"Girl, there is nothing to forgive. I know you have had a lot to deal with. But if I can get back to my story, please," she said, rolling her eyes and continuing with her story. She told her friends how she and Jon had been working together to get things together for the anniversary and how he'd asked her out on a date. That's why she couldn't go walking with them today. Jon was going to take her to see all the hot Atlanta tourist attractions, starting with the Georgia Aquarium. They were supposed to be meeting there at eleven o'clock.

"I was going to say that you are looking exceptionally pulchritudinous today," Devine laughed.

"What?" The girls said at the same time and the group broke out in raucous laughter.

Devine continued, "I'm serious. You ladies are stunning. Especially you Symone, with that new Brazilian hair."

They all laughed again.

Even though Symone had gone off on a mild tangent, the morning progressed without any further incidence but there was a bit of underlying tension as a result of her unspoken accusations.

At ten thirty, the group disbanded. Jynx headed to the aquarium. Devine met up with Cha-Cha to do Lord knows what and Symone walked to the park. Alone. She needed to clear her head and try to figure out why she was acting the way she was. Keyon really was a good man and she was very fortunate to have him in her life. But lately, she was not as happy as she should have been and it wasn't his fault. Something was missing inside of her but she couldn't determine exactly what it was. *Mama, I wish you were here to help me with this. I really need you*, she thought.

Several people were out tossing around Frisbees, walking dogs and flying kites. Symone wished she had brought a good book to read. She loved reading and remembered a few books she'd picked up from the Book Fair. Symone would get to it this evening because she knew she wouldn't have anything else on her agenda.

Since yesterday morning, she and Keyon had not spoken one word to one another. He even moved his things into the guest bedroom down the hall. *I know you can't stand being in the same room with me so God forbid you have to share a bed with me too,* he said. She still couldn't believe that she said that to him. She sat down on a bench under a huge tree. It hid her with its shade. Deep in thought, she didn't hear the stranger approach her.

"Nickel for your thoughts?" the person asked.

"Huh? A nickel? I thought it was 'a penny for your thoughts'?" she replied.

"Okay," the person said, pulling a penny out, handing it to her, "if that's all your thoughts are worth, here you go." For the first time in ages, a genuine smile spread across her face.

"Uh, thanks. You're so silly, uh...?"

"Donita. But you can call me, Donnie," the woman answered.

"Oh, you're a wom-...? I mean to say...shit! I'm sorry. It seems I've been fucking up all day so far."

"Don't sweat it, Ma. You have nothing to apologize for. It happens all the time. But I'm a woman."

"So, are you gay? Wow! I can't believe I just asked that. I have a distinct taste of a foot in my mouth," Symone said, embarrassed.

Laughing, Donnie said, "I'm a lesbian if that's what you wanna know. I don't really like the word 'gay'. I just do what I do, and I do that very well."

"I'll bet you do," she said eyeing the sexy androgynous woman, before she caught herself. "Did I say that out loud, too? Aw naw, hell naw, I done up and done it. Let me leave before I say something else to embarrass myself. Please forgive me. I'm not usually like this," Symone said, getting up to leave.

"Please don't leave. You're fine, Ma. Really. But one thing I been waiting for you to say is your name."

"See? Just plain old rude, I am. Symone. Symone Morrow," she said, offering the woman her hand.

"No, shit? Are you the radio host?" Symone nodded her head affirmatively. "Wow, I can't believe it. I listen to your show all the time."

"Really? How wonderful."

"Yeah, I guess you can say I'm a fan."

Symone smiled. She asked Donnie what had brought her to the park and Donnie told her that she was just trying to clear her head.

"Same here. I have a lot going on," she admitted.

"Sounds like it. You wanna talk about it?" Donnie asked, concerned.

34

"I wouldn't want to burden you. And it's not cool to un-load my problems on a complete stranger."

"Aren't you the one always saying that sometimes it's best to talk to someone who is impartial to what's going on in your life?"

"Well, you really are a fan, huh?"

"And you know this. Now tell Dr. D what's going on."

For the next hour Symone talked and Donnie just listened. She spoke of what was going on with her job, her relationship with her friends, and even Keyon and their pending nuptials. She even admitted how jealous she had become when she thought that it was Keyon who was messing around in his studio.

"It was such a bad night for me. He didn't show up to my event and I felt neglected. I had no idea he had been hurt but when I asked him about it, he refused to tell me. Things have been so haywire. I took my engagement ring off the other day and set it on a soap dish in the bathroom and now it's gone. I think it fell down the drain. I've been wearing this one just so Keyon wouldn't notice my finger was bare."

"You lost your ring?"

"Yep and the crazy part is that I don't really care. I know it cost a small mint 'cause it was a 5 carat pear shaped diamond ring by Harry Winston."

"Damn, that nigga must love yo' ass a lot to drop that kind of cash on you."

"Money is cool, but I want something more than that. Something that he ain't giving me."

"Sounds like you got it all to me."

"Not everything."

"Look, I know we just met and all so forgive me if I'm overstepping my bounds, but it sounds to me that things started getting crazy for you and your fiancé after he proposed. Do you think that you may have commitment issues?"

"I don't think so. He and I have been together for five years and he is the only man I have been with in that time. Nah, commitment is not an issue for me or him."

"I think that's the issue. Even though you two have been together so long, marriage is something totally different from just being boyfriend and girlfriend. That's permanent. Or at least it's supposed to be."

"You know, as crazy as it seems, you may be on to something. Come to think of it, I didn't start acting strange until a few months ago. And every time he talks about setting a date, I go off on him. Yep, you are definitely on to something. Thanks."

"No problem. Anything I can do to help, I will."

All of a sudden the sky opened up and rain poured down hard. Donnie and Symone, as with all the park goers, were caught unawares. Donnie took her shirt off and covered Symone's head. She had a white wife beater on under the navy crew neck t-shirt she had on. Symone was caught off guard by the chivalrous gesture but was pleased nonetheless. When the masculine woman pulled Symone close to her to keep her shielded from the rain, a charge coursed through her. Donnie, who stood eight inches taller than Symone's five feet-four inch frame, looked down into her eyes. Their faces were only about an inch apart as they huddled together under the tree.

Symone's lips parted.

Donnie's head dipped lower.

Symone stood on her tiptoes.

Donnie's lips came close.

Barely, just barely, had their lips grazed one another's but sparks flew. Symone's clitoris jumped like a grasshopper. Donnie deepened the kiss and put her hand under Symone's chin, drawing her closer to her. A soft moan escaped Symone's lips. A couple running out of the park to seek shelter screamed "get a room" on their way past the couple, ending the magic moment.

"Damn. I'm so sorry, Symone. I know that you have a man and you're not into women like that. Please forgive me. I didn't mean to disrespect you."

She berated herself in such a way that made Symone feel bad. She knew the other woman didn't plan to kiss her. It was just something that happened. But it was clear that the other woman was feeling pretty badly about it. Oddly enough, Symone didn't feel disrespected by the kiss at all. As a matter of fact, she had quite enjoyed it. But she couldn't tell the other woman that, could she? Would that encourage her? Make her think she was into her or any woman for that matter? Symone remembered how she and some of her college friends used to talk about lesbians. They used to call them such harsh names like, dyke, carpet munchers and bull-daggers. Was she one of them now? She had enjoyed that kiss and until it ended abruptly and she was looking forward to seeing what Donnie could do with that tongue of hers. And even more perplexing to her was that she had never experienced a sensation like that with Keyon. Ever.

Confused, Symone cleared her throat. "You didn't disrespect me. Not at all. Let's just forget about it, shall we?"

"Alright. Um, would you like to grab a bite to eat? My treat?" Donnie offered.

"I just ate breakfast a half hour ago," Symone replied.

"Do you know what time it is? We've been sitting on the bench talking for almost four hours before the rain started. It's almost three o'clock."

"Wow. Time really got away from me. Well then in that case, lead the way."

Donnie led Symone to her car and drove a few blocks south to Ponce De Leon and parked by the Spaghetti Factory. It was a casual place that served good food and after driving the short distance, both woman's stomachs began growling.

"I guess we are hungry," Symone giggled.

Inside the restaurant, the hostess showed the women to a private booth at the back of the establishment. They ordered their meals and picked up their conversation where it had left off in the park. Before the kiss.

Symone told Donnie about Keyon's upcoming event. She told her that it was going to be held at the same hotel where her awards banquet was held. For the next three hours the two of them chatted away like old friends.

"This is so cool."

"What is?"

"This. Being here with you and finally being able to talk about Keyon and me without everyone trying to shove his great qualities down my throat. I was just saying the other day that I wanted a friend who just knew me. A friend all to myself."

"So we're friends now, are we?"

"Yes ma'am. I think that you and I needed to meet today. It was fate."

"You got that right, Ma."

Donnie shared with Symone a little about her life. She told her that like Symone, she only had one relative, her brother. Their grandparents and father raised them after their mom left. Her mom, who was a waitress, abandoned them when she was two so she had no clear memories of her. Damian, who was five by the time she left, could at least remember what she looked like. Their dad, who tried his best to raise them, didn't have a clue what to do, so he moved them all in with his parents. He never did tell them why their mom left them. Donnie told her that her life, for the most part, was good and that she didn't have any regrets. She and her brother, who were very close, had some great times together. A couple of years ago, her grandfather had died in his sleep of natural causes. Then a week later, her grandmother had followed him on to glory.

"They said she died of a broken heart. We were sad, but they lived good lives. Treated everyone well and loved us as much as they could. Our dad took it harder than we did."

"How old were they?"

"Granddad was 96 and Grandma was 95."

"Wow. Well the Word does say 'with long life will I satisfy him'. I hope I find a love that lasts like that."

"You don't think that you have that now?"

"Honestly, I don't know. I said some hurtful things to Keyon the other day, things I didn't even know were in me, and I don't mean to get all preachy but again, the Word says 'out of the abundance of the heart does the mouth speak.' That's why a drunken tongue speaks a sober heart. They just tell what they really have been feeling."

"So, you think that you really can't stand your man? Straight up?" Donnie asked incredulously.

"I love him, but I get so tired of people telling me how fucking lucky I am to be with him. Like, why can't he be lucky to be with me? Hell, I am just as popular as he is. I mean, no, I don't have millions of dollars in my bank account like he does, but hell I do pretty well for myself. Everyone, even Devine, thinks he is so fucking perfect. No one thinks his ass can do any wrong. It's like the sun rises and sets in his ass. Ugh!" She let out an angry sigh.

"Exhale, Ma. It's all good here. With me, it's all about you, babe. You're fucking perfect," Donnie said as she placed her hand over Symone's and gently caressed it. "I never met a woman like you in my life. You're beautiful, smart and classy. If you were mine, I would drink your dirty bathwater every night."

Symone felt like she was the center of attention and she reveled in it. Donnie treated her like a princess and even though Symone wasn't feeling her in that way, she knew she needed everything that Donnie was offering her at that moment.

Forty-five minutes later, Donnie dropped a smiling Symone off in front of her Buckhead home and drove off into the sunset. Her phone was hot. Charmaine had been texting and calling all day but she ignored her. She would deal with her later. Donnie scrolled through her contacts and placed a call. Sunday or not, someone would pick up.

"First Class Staffing, Angel speaking."

"Hey Angel, this is, Donnie."

The receptionist softened on the other end of the line. "Hey, Donnie. I was wondering when you were going to call me. I've been missing you, Boo."

"Yo, I been missing your sexy ass, too, Angel. Matter of fact, I wanna see you tonight. A nigga dick getting hard just hearing your sexy ass voice."

"Okay. I'm at home right now so you can come over. I have the office phones transferred here 'cause I didn't feel like staying there all day to answer phones that may not ring."

"Must be nice to work for your mom's company."

"It's cool. How long will it be before you get here? I need to shower and shit."

"I should touch down 'bout fifteen minutes. But yo', check this out, do you all handle all the staffing for the W Perimeter? You know the joint you sent me to the other night?"

"Yes. We have a contract with them. Why?"

"Well you know a nigga like me trying to break into the music biz and shit and I just found out Man of Steel Records is having their fifth anniversary bash there. I figure if I can get in, I will have a chance to get my demo over to one of the execs."

"Oh, baby you are such a genius. Mama said they were having the party there, but it slipped my mind. Of course I will make sure that you are one of the servers. I got you."

"I know you do. And Angel?"

"Yes, Donnie."

"Come to the door naked." Then she closed her phone.

# What's Done In The Dark

Some people just wouldn't let her be nice to them. Charmaine realized that now. So from that moment on it was no more Ms. Nice Girl. Every move she made would be carefully thought out and planned. About four weeks ago, she had sent a small hint to a chick that Donnie had fucked, Vanessa Lester, a pretty hostess who worked at Houston's on Peachtree Street. The girl had let Donnie finger her on the sofa, but they hadn't gone any further than that. Not at Donnie's house anyway. When she left Donnie's place, her car was damaged as a result of a hit and run. Charmaine knew that she should have done something more than that, but at the time she was too angry to think straight. She knew that the little ding set Vanessa back almost $600 because it was by her gas tank.

But it was evident that the chick didn't get the point because she was with Donnie again and this time, she went too far. Not only was Vanessa with her, they had an unidentified woman with them. They weren't making lots of noise but the sensitive microphones near the bed alerted Charmaine that someone was in the room. She woke up just in time to see Vanessa suck the other girl's breasts while Donnie looked on in fascination. The nameless chick pulled Donnie close to her and started tonguing her down. Vanessa lifted the girl's mini skirt and squealed with delight when she saw the woman had no panties on. She continued to suck on her titties and finger her at the same time. Even from a distance, Charmaine could hear how wet the woman was as Vanessa's fingers moved in and out, making slurping noises.

Within seconds all three of the women were totally naked and Charmaine was sitting ramrod straight watching the scene play out below her, getting angry and turned on simultaneously.

The nameless chick laid Vanessa down on the bed and began to suck on her toes, nibbling each one, slowly making her way up her inner thigh. Once her mouth found the heated center, her tongue flicked the hard bud and Vanessa squirmed. She moaned as the woman licked her and sucked on her clit aggressively. Donnie, who obviously didn't want to be left out of the action, put her face between Jane Doe's thighs and began to fuck her pussy with her tongue. Vanessa then helped Donnie move closer to her so that she could she suck on the dick that Donnie wore. It was an almost perfect circle of fucking and sucking. Charmaine's own pussy was wet and her clit ached painfully with the need to be touched. While keeping her eyes on the screen, she inserted two fingers in her pussy and began to massage her clit with her thumb. Her hips gyrated on the floor and she pumped faster, creating the right amount of friction to cum just as the ladies below her did.

Tiny beads of sweat formed on Charmaine's forehead while she was cuming and she wiped them off after she sucked her juices from her fingers. Below, Jane Doe moved to sit on Donnie's face, grinding her pussy in circular motions in the woman's mouth as Vanessa knelt between Donnie's legs and sucked the silicone dick while fingering herself. Jane came in Donnie's mouth and kissed her so deeply afterwards, that it looked like Donnie had swallowed her tongue. There were almost twelve hidden cameras in the room and Charmaine was getting the action from every angle possible. Donnie told Jane to get on her knees and she came up behind her with some lubricant and lubed her now condom covered strap-on and Jane's ass hole. She spread her ass cheeks apart and slowly slid the tool inside. Jane Doe yelped in pain but soon adjusted and then buried her mouth into Vanessa's snatch to pleasure the other woman. Donnie looked down as she moved in and out slowly. When she picked up the pace, Jane made her ass clap turning Donnie on even more. Vanessa had long since came and was now beside Donnie, licking her nipples and playing in her own wetness.

"Dammit baby, this dick feels so good in my ass. I want you all up in me! Fuck me, Don Juan. Tear this ass up!"

"You want me to tear it up? Take all this dick then you nasty bitch!"

Charmaine, who was now satisfied, looked on in anger and the let it completely envelop her. She smiled and nodded as the voices in her head told her what she could do to show that bitch once and for all what was up. It might take a little investigating, but she would find out who Jane Doe was and she would show her, too. The camera's recorded the show below but Charmaine had enough. She didn't know how long the three women fucked because she muted the sound, turned off the monitors and went to sleep. She could always rewind it.

Donnie was not going to change. Of that, Charmaine was sure. Just yesterday at lunchtime, Donnie had called her cell phone and told her how much she loved and missed her. Although she was happy when she saw her ex's face pop up on her phone, she was sad at the same time. Donnie was her first and only female lover. She'd turned her out on her 21st birthday five years ago while she was in Atlanta checking out the medical school at Emory University. They'd been messing around off and on since then.

Charmaine moved from California to Atlanta in order to be closer to her because; that is what Donnie said she wanted. They were supposed to go to New York to get married and then honeymoon in The Hamptons, but none of that came to pass. Shortly after Charmaine arrived in Georgia, Donnie changed. She kept her isolated most of the time and treated her badly. They hardly ever went out or did anything and when they did, it was only with Donnie's friends. Donnie told Charmaine what to wear, what to eat, where to go and when to bathe. It was as if she was in prison and her girlfriend was the warden.

Damian, Donnie's brother, was the one who told Charmaine that she needed to get out of the relationship. He'd witnessed one too many fights and often had been the one to take her to the hospital when she needed it. But she was alone in a strange city and the only person she knew was Donnie so she always came back.

Of course, Donnie would apologize and tell her that she loved her and how it would never happen again, and for a while things would be cool. Then one day, something as petty as a fly in the house would set Donnie off and she would wail on Charmaine. Their last fight had left Charmaine with a black eye and hairline fractured ribs. The police, who were smarter than Charmaine, had refused to let her leave with her alleged abuser and had taken her to a domestic violence shelter. For ninety days, she learned about power and control, the two main components of domestic violence and she learned about herself.

By the time she exited the shelter, she had a completely different outlook on life. The shelter staff helped her find a good job and they also assisted her with housing so that she didn't have to return to Donnie's. It wasn't long after she got settled into her new place that Donnie came knocking again, and of course Charmaine took her back. She needed to believe that the first and probably only woman that she ever loved had truly loved her in return and wasn't just using her. The young, naïve girl that Donnie had turned out was gone. The blinders were off. And the threesome that Donnie had just participated in really had her seeing things more clearly than ever before.

After Donnie and her party left, Charmaine went home to check on some things. She sent Donnie a text to check on her.

*"Hey babe, wyd?"*

*"Not shit. @ the gym working out."*

Charmaine read the lie and shook her head. *"Is that right. U getting it in, huh?"*

*"Yeah U know how I do it."*

*"Alright then, well I'll let U get 2 it. R we still on 4 2nite?"*

*"Yep, yep. Can't wait. Been a minute since I nutted. I need U, Char. ILY."*

*"ILY2."*

Disgusted, Charmaine made her way to the backyard of her house. As she walked further out, she began to hear the streaming water in her Koi Pond that she had installed a month ago. Foresight had told her that she would need special tools for the bitches that Donnie fucked with. The small shed faced in an East-West direction to reduce direct sunlight from coming through. Her babies needed a dark, dank, well-vegetated habitat.

The raw steaks that she used for an attractant were long gone and the few flies that she captured had done a superb job. Once she went inside the shed, she could hear the creepy crawlers feasting off the raw chickens she had placed inside their screen-covered tanks days ago. She was actually surprised that there was anything left on the bones, but she knew that would help fertilize more bugs. Using a metal ice scooper, she unlatched the lid and scooped four large heaps into a lidded container. She put the lid back on, made sure it was secure and left.

• • • • • • • • • • • • • • • • •

Vanessa Lester got out of her car and headed into the Fit and Fine Gym with a huge smile on her face. Donnie had just sent her a text and told her that she'd never felt for anyone the way she did about her. Hopefully after last night, Donnie would see that Vanessa cared deeply about her too. The threesome that they had was Donnie's idea and Vanessa didn't want to do it at first but her lover told her that would prove to her once and for all where her heart was, so Vanessa conceded. She was glad that she did, too. It was fun and she came longer and harder than ever before. Now it was time to work out so that could maintain the sexy body that Donnie loved so much. For two hours she ran, lifted, twisted and swam until she was tired. After thirty minutes in the sauna, she showered, dressed and left the gym.

Approaching her car, she saw a white envelope tucked behind the windshield wiper. She opened it and read the note inside.

"There's more than one way to skin a cat," she read out loud. "What in the hell is this bullshit?"

The car chirped when she hit the unlock button and popped the trunk. She threw her purse and cell phone into the front passenger's seat then walked a couple of steps to the trunk. She got ready to throw her bag inside when she saw what looked like blood drip. Slowly she looked into the trunk until she saw her cat Fluffy, lying in the trunk, skinned, with a knife through her heart. Vanessa screamed in anguish and hurried to get her phone to call the cops. When she sat in the front seat she immediately smelled a foul odor, which was exacerbated by the heat. Out of habit, she lifted the armrest to grab the small bottle of orange scented car freshener.

Not paying attention, her hand landed on something slimy. When she looked down, maggots were on her skin and hundreds of them covered a dead fish. She turned her head to find her hair stuck to the seat. But she could lean forward a bit and saw that there were hundreds more in the back seat, hungrily feasting on raw meat. She screamed and struggled to get out of the car but the door was stuck. She banged on the window and tried to pry the door open, but it didn't budge. Moments later, a man passing by saw her struggling and came over to help. He pulled and couldn't get the door open either.

"Hold on, I'm going to call 9-1-1."

"Don't leave me! Please help me. Break the glass. Just get me out of here!"

The man went to his car to get a crow bar and ran back to her car. "Turn your head and cover your eyes," he told her before smashing the window. He tried to pull her out of the car, but noticed her hair was stuck. "I'm going to have to cut your hair or else it will rip."

"This is weave. Do what you gotta do. Just please get me out of here!"

"Are you okay? What happened?" he asked, pulling a switch blade from his pocket.

"Someone killed my cat. She's in the trunk dead,"

Vanessa cried. "I got in the car to call the police and then couldn't get out."

The man looked at her and then inside the car and shook his head in disbelief after cutting the weave, leaving pieces stuck to the seat. He then made his way to the trunk. His stomach rolled violently when he saw the cat. He called the cops and waited until they arrived and filed a report. The rookie cop had seen some strange things since he joined the force but this took the cake. He took the note and said he would turn it in when he got back to the station along with the report and then called a tow truck and had it towed to the police station. Vanessa didn't know who had written the note, but it scared her enough that she didn't leave the house. Whoever it was that sent that note, Vanessa got the message loud and clear.

• • • • • • • • • • • • • • • • • •

Monday, Keyon told his assistant to hold all of his calls and cancel all of the day's appointments. He didn't want to talk to nor see anyone. The texts and calls were coming more frequently now and he was at his wits end. His mood was black and the staff at M.O.S. could tell. An intern left out of his office in tears after he chewed her out for bringing him a lukewarm cup of coffee. Judy, who was like a second mom, came in to set him straight.

"Now. I don't know what the hell is wrong with you, but boss or no boss, you will not mistreat anyone here on my watch. You got that, buddy?"

"I'm sorry, Judy. Please tell her I'm sorry. I just have a lot on my mind, that's all."

"I can see that. Is it Symone?"

"Among other things."

*Keyon thought back to the beating that took place the night of Symone's big event. He wished like hell that he could tell her the truth. He really did want her to know why he'd gotten beat and ended up with bruised ribs. One day he would tell her that night was no accident. Big's men meant to punish his body and ego, sending him a message. He also wanted to share with her the fact that business wasn't going as well as she thought it was.*

"Baby, a blind man can see something is wrong between you two," Judy stated, moving closer to his face.

Keyon clearly wasn't giving Judy his undivided attention.

"She's not wearing her engagement ring anymore. Did you guys call the wedding off?"

Although he hadn't called the wedding off, he *had* taken the ring back. He needed the money to pay a debt. Symone had no clue. When he got things in order, he would buy her a bigger, better set.

"No, we didn't call the wedding off. But she refuses to set a date. Shit, I thought we would have jumped the broom by now. I don't think she wants to marry me."

"Not every lady feels that she needs a ring, or a man to validate her existence as a woman. Maybe Symone is one of those and just too scared to tell you."

"I don't know. None of this makes sense. Lately, all she does is accuse me of cheating on her, and the other day she said she stayed away from home intentionally because she couldn't stand being in the same room as me. What kind of shit is that?"

"Listen, Keyon. You're like a son to me, and Lord knows I hate to see you like this. Why don't you try romancing her? Take her some flowers and candy and ask her out on a date. Rekindle the fire that you all once had. Talk to one another and see what's on her mind. Stop trying to figure out what's wrong. Just ask her. That's the only way you'll last. Honest communication is the key."

"You're right. Let me stop feeling sorry myself and go win my woman back."

"That's the spirit. Well, I'm off to meet my other son. He's taking me to dinner."

"Should I be jealous that you are adopting more kids?"

"There's no need, baby boy. You will always be my first son. Love you. Now, get outta here."

Ten minutes later, Keyon stopped by the flower shop and picked up a dozen yellow roses for Symone, a box of chocolates and some perfume. He was going to show her how much she meant to him. It had been a minute since they had made love and he was going to make her remember all the reasons she fell in love with him.

When he got home, she wasn't there yet so he showered and relaxed awaiting her return. An hour had passed and she hadn't called nor texted. Bored, he got up and decided to do a little work until she got in. Her laptop was on her nightstand and he leaned over and grabbed it so he could check his email. Symone's instant messenger was still up and the last conversation she had was in plain sight. He knew that her I/M name was Moniluv but who was Don Juan? Was Symone cheating on him? Is that why she was always accusing him, because she was doing it herself? He shook his head and read the exchange.

*Moniluv: Thx so much 4 dinner the other night. I really enjoyed myself. It's been a long time.*

*Don Juan: You're welcome, love. It's been a long time 4 what babe?*

*Moniluv: Among other things, good conversation. J*

*Don Juan: So what u saying, Ma? Ur pretty pussy ain't been wet?*

*Moniluv: Not in almost a month. L*

*Don Juan: Well we're going 2 have 2 do something about that now aren't we?*

*Moniluv: Listen @ u. Don't tempt me.*

*Don Juan: So I'm tempting, huh?*

*Moniluv: Yeah. I hate 2 admit it but u r. That scares me 2.*

*Don Juan: Don't b scared, Ma. I got u. I'd never do u like he does. Ur a fucking princess right now but I'd treat u like a queen.*

*Moniluv: I bet u would 2. But I'm not ready 4 that right*

*now. Keyon is a good man.*

**Don Juan**: *That's all good, Ma. But I can b better 2 u than him any day of the week. All I'm asking 4 is a chance 2 show u.*

**Moniluv:** *I can't cheat. He's been faithful 2 me.*

**Don Juan**: *But u have ur doubts. No worries, Ma. Like I told u the other day. I'm here 4 u. I ain't going nowhere. I can't lie, I want ur ass 2 b my woman bad, but not bad enuf 2 ruin our friendship. Ur way 2 important 2 do that.*

**Moniluv**: *Thx, D. that means a lot 2 me right now. I will ttyl. I gotta take my ass 2 work & I still need 2 shower.*

**Don Juan**: *Damn!*

**Don Juan**: *My dick just hard thinking about u naked. Shit! J*

**Moniluv**: *Roflmao! Bye Silly.*

**Don Juan**: *Later, Ma!*

Keyon closed the computer. There was no way he was getting married until Symone gave him some answers. When she came in from work he was going to hit her with the five words that most men hated to hear, "Baby, we need to talk."

# Best Laid Plans

It was time to call in her markers, a couple of them anyway. For what Donnie had planned, she knew the two people to redeem favors from; Chante DuLac and Domynique Segar. Chante was a pharmacist at CVS and could get her what she needed, Rohypnol and Lithium; an odd combination of drugs, but very necessary for her mission.

In public, Chante was a staunch and polished professional and the wife of a Georgia mayor. But in private, she was a pussy-licking nympho who loved when Donnie gave it to her in the ass. Together, the two of them participated in some very raunchy sex parties. Parties that Donnie was sure the husband was not aware of. During one of their raunchier times together, Donnie had taped Chante getting fucked with a two-prong strap-on.

Donnie kept the tape to use for financial gain but soon found out it wouldn't take all that. She was so sprung off the tongue that all Donnie had to do was lick that spot and the woman would submit and give her anything she asked for. Donnie looked at her watch and saw that it was almost two-thirty. Chante would be available to talk. Donnie grabbed her cell phone off her nightstand, dialed, and waited patiently while the call was connected.

"This is Chante."

"What's up Tay-Tay? This is Stone."

"Baby, I'm so glad you called me. I was just thinking about you."

"Is that right? And what were you thinking?"

"Oh, just how I would love to feel your big dick ramming into my ass, while you finger my pussy. I want to cum all over your hard dick, Stone. And if you hit it from the back like you love to, you can see all the cream from my pussy. Don't you want it baby?"

"Shit, I'm stroking my dick now just thinking about you. We can get together tonight if you have the time. But yo, check it. A nigga like me needs you to do something. I need some Rohypnol and Lithium. Can you do that for me, babe?"

"Rohypnol and Lithium? You're making a Mindless Mickey? Hmm, out of it enough to not realize what's going on, but lucid enough to enjoy it. You're a dirty bird, Stone, but I got you. You know it's gonna cost you though?"

"Oh yeah, how much?"

"The husband is going to a conference in D.C. It's for three boring ass days and he's making me go with him. If I have to go, so do you."

"Three days with you in the Chocolate City? Oh, hell yeah. Just say the word and baby I'm there."

"Wonderful. Meet me at our usual spot at 9:30 p.m. I'll bring what you need tonight."

"Cool. Tonight it is then. Peace." Once that call was finished, Donnie dialed the next one.

"May I please speak to Domynique?"

"Speaking."

"Darling, Nikki. How in the hell have you been?"

The other woman cringed on the other end at the mentioning of her nickname before she answered. "I'm okay, Stone. How are you?"

"I'm cool. You remember that favor you owe me? Well, I'm calling to collect on it."

"The favor? I uh, well, I thought that since it's been so long that maybe you would have umm…"

"You thought I would have forgotten? Thought I would have let you off the hook? You *are* stupid, huh? Now why in the hell would I let a lying, no account thief off the hook? By the way, did you ever pay back the $700 I caught you stealing from Saks?" There was silence on the other end. "Well did you? Don't get quiet now."

"I haven't had the money to pay it back yet, Stone. But I promise I will. I always pay my debts. I'm really not a thief; I tried to tell you that before. I just needed the money so that I could put my sister away nicely. I didn't want her to be buried in a pine box."

"Sniff, sniff. Like I care what you stole the money for. I took my job as the manager of asset protection seriously and you tried to jeopardize my position with the company. So to make sure that you never tried no bullshit like that again, I got your ass on tape taking that money. I still have that tape, too. Both of 'em now that I think about it."

"B-b-both of them?"

"Yes, ma'am. One of you stealing and one of you cumming in my mouth. My tongue felt good in that wet box didn't it? Your pussy tasted like honey. How did you do that? I still ain't never had no pussy like yours. It was so tight my tongue could hardly penetrate you let alone my fingers. Shit, I want some of that right now. My dick is hard. Too bad for you I got somewhere else to be, otherwise I would tear that pussy up," she said massaging her strap-on through her jeans.

"Please don't turn me in to the cops or show that other tape to anyone, Stone. I will do whatever you ask."

"That's exactly what I wanted to hear. I need you to fuck this nigga for me. I will have a room and everything set up. It's going down Labor Day Weekend. You just make sure that a nigga like me don't have to come hunting yo' ass down. And keep your phone on. I don't care what you have to do or whose dick you have to suck to get the money but when I call, your ass better answer, or there will be hell to pay. You feel me?"

"Yes, Stone. I understand."

"Good. I'll talk to you soon." Donnie hung up her phone and rolled onto her back on her bed. Turned on by the way things were shaping up, she pulled her pants down to stroke her dick, moaning in pleasure. Her cell phone vibrated and she looked at the text message that just came in. *I wanna see you baby. Come give me that big ass dick of yours. My pussy is wet and waiting.* Donnie replied *"gimme an hour. I have one stop to make."*

● ● ● ● ● ● ● ● ● ● ● ● ● ● ● ● ● ●

Charmaine watched Donnie closely in the monitor after sending that text. She knew that Donnie was up to no good. *Why would Donnie want Rohypnol?* Charmaine pondered. Her woman was always so good at sweet talking other women. Charmaine didn't know much about Lithium except that most people who had Bi-Polar Disorder took it. But the two drugs as a combination? Who knew? *But I will find out. I have got to keep my eyes on her*, she thought as she wrote down the names of the women Donnie just spoke to.

There was a camera situated in the light globe directly above the bed so Charmaine was able to zoom in on her girl-friends face. She took note of the glazed over maniacal look that her eyes held, and the slow, creepy way that she nodded her head like she was agreeing with someone. *The voices in her head probably...and people call me psycho.* When Donnie tilted her head to the left, Charmaine was able to see a very fresh hickey on her neck, noting that it was not there the day before. Speaking out loud, she said, "I know you must have done that Symone. And since you want to play, I got something for your ass, too." An hour later, Donnie got up and left the house and Charmaine followed suit less than ten minutes later.

By the time Donnie made it to Charmaine's, she had been home 45 minutes. *This bitch has no regard for time.* Charmaine opened the door and welcomed Donnie with a kiss on the lips.

"Somebody's happy to see me," Donnie said.

"I'm always happy to see you."

"I'll be the judge of that," Donnie said, sliding her fin-

54

gers in Charmaine's shorts and dipping them in her pussy. It was wet. "Yep. Assume the position."

Without hesitation, Charmaine dropped to her knees and began to suck Donnie's man-made dick. She was used to the strap-on, and sucked it like a real dick.

"Awe shit, Char. Take this dick down your throat. Awe, you know how I like it." Donnie put both of her hands on Charmaine's head and guided her moves. Ten minutes later, she had Charmaine bent over the edge of the sofa, fucking her doggystyle. Donnie spread her cheeks apart so that she could see the cream on her dick as she went in and out. Charmaine played with her clit while Donnie rammed her, helping to create the best orgasm she had had in ages.

"Donnie, baby. I-am-cum-ming!" She screeched as her body released its juices. Donnie slowly pulled out and sat on the sofa, pulling Charmaine up to her body and holding her.

"Where did you get that hickey on your neck, Donita?" Charmaine asked.

"I'on know what'chu talking about."

"The hickey on the left side of your neck. The one I didn't put there."

Angry, Donnie pulled Charmaine's hair and turned her around to face her. "This is why I don't like fucking with your punk ass. You can't never just let us be happy. Always gotta say some slick shit to spoil the mood. I keep telling yo' ass I ain't fucking nobody else. That's a damn acid burn I got at one of my temp jobs. I was cleaning exhaust fans."

"Why are you always lying to me," Charmaine cried. "I know you be fucking other bitches and I know about that fuckin' DJ. I'm gonna fuck'em all up. I swear I am."

Donnie didn't respond. Instead, she jumped off the sofa and backhanded Charmaine so hard she flipped over the arm of the sofa. Before she got up, Donnie was on her, punching her in the head. Out of breath, Donnie got up and headed for the door after fixing her clothes.

"I'm out. Call me when you ready to apologize."

"No, baby. Please don't go. I'm sorry. Donnie, please," Charmaine begged, dropping to the floor, and holding on to Donnie's ankle.

"Bitch, get off me," she said, kicking Charmaine off. "I got shit to do. And I don't care what you do, but don't you lay a hand on 'Mone, she's special. And then she slammed the door behind her. Charmaine put her hand on the door as if feeling for Donnie and cried herself to sleep.

● ● ● ● ● ● ● ● ● ● ● ● ● ● ● ● ● ●

Keyon sat in the living room and waited for Symone to come down stairs. A few days had passed since he read the instant messages and he still hadn't cooled off. His plan was to talk to her the same night, but she didn't come in until after he'd fallen asleep. When he woke up the next day, she was already gone. This was the first time he would have an opportunity to talk things over with her. He heard her heals click cross the granite tile in the foyer of their home and called out to her.

"Symone, can you come in here for minute?"

"What is it, babe? I'm on my way to meet Jynx for lunch. You know how I hate tardiness."

"Yeah, when it comes to your friends or work," he mumbled under his breath.

"What did you say?"

"Nothing. Look, we need to talk. The other day when I waited for you to get home, I decided to do some work and I used your laptop. I saw some inst..."

"I'm sorry babe, hold that thought," she said and answered her ringing cell phone.

"Symone..." Keyon tried again.

"Talk to me. What? Really? Say no more, I'm on my way." She ended the call and tossed the phone in her bag.

"No, we need to talk now." Keyon demanded this time.

"Keyon, can we save this until later? That was my producer. Some Radio Ten execs are at the station and wanna talk to me. I gotta go." She kissed him on the cheek before running out of the house.

Keyon shook his head in disbelief. "Ain't that a bitch?" he asked to the empty room. Their talk would have to wait a little while longer. His phone vibrated and he looked at the text message. *Get my money soon or else you will be planning a funeral instead of a wedding.*

# Who Can You Run To

"That's right Atlanta, you heard it here first. The Man of Steele Records Five Year Anniversary Bash will be going down Labor Day Weekend. I have two, grand prizes to give away which includes two VIP tickets to the event for each winner, a chauffeur driven car to get you to the party in style and $500 cash. That'll help somebody look fresh to death. Starting tomorrow, be the 11th caller after hearing *Get That*, the new single from SKY-Hi and you will be entered to win one of the two grand prizes. My time is up folks. This is your favorite show 'Symone Says' and this is your favorite host, Symone Morrow, reminding you all to be good or be good at it."

Dread and trepidation filled Symone as she gathered her belongings and prepared to leave the station for the evening. She still had not spoken to Keyon and had been avoiding every attempt that he made to speak with her. It was only a matter of time before she had to face the music but tonight really wasn't the night. All she wanted to do was take a hot shower and hit the sack. Whatever Keyon wanted to talk about could surely wait. Couldn't it? Hell, it had waited this long, a few more days wouldn't hurt. Lately, so many things hadn't been going Symone's way. Her relationship with her friends was strained because of her refusal to deal with the situation with Keyon. She hated that they were *her* friends yet obviously sided with him. That's why she was so happy to have Donnie in her life now.

Donnie got her. She understood things that no one else

did, and when they were together she would allow Symone to vent and listened patiently. Since the first kiss, 'barely kiss' they shared, Donnie hadn't tried to kiss or make a move on her again, much to Symone's chagrin. It was weird to her, because even though she wasn't into women, she was into Donnie. But then, Donnie was not your typical woman. She was easily somewhere in between male and female, leaning more to the male side. Regardless of how anyone else saw her, Symone was beginning to see Donnie in a different way. They were friends, but lately, Symone had been longing for something more with the other woman. She was lost in thought when the night security walked up to her holding a package.

"This came for you, Ms. Morrow. I'm getting ready to make my rounds and thought I'd drop it off or else I may forget to give it you."

"Thank you, Burt. I appreciate you. Have a great night."

"You too, ma'am."

It was the same size box she'd been getting for weeks. It was wrapped in the same brown paper. Symone was sure that it was another bald headed Barbie Doll. She snickered as she began to unwrap it, thinking about the strange person who kept sending her the dolls. This box was lighter than the others, but she still placed it on her desk and sat down so that she could get a good look at what her secret admirer had sent her this week. When she opened the box, Jennifer, an intern for the station came over to see what she had received. Symone jumped when the young lady started screaming at the top of her lungs. The security guard came running towards the two women to see what the commotion was all about. Symone just sat there speechless, visibly shaken, shaking her head at the contents of the box.

Burt looked at the box and yelled out, "What the fuck is that?"

By now, a crowd had gathered and everyone was murmuring about the 'gift'.

"There's a note glued inside the box top," Burt noticed.

"What does it say?" Someone asked.

*"Since you wanna act like a fucking chicken head, I thought you might like one of your own, bitch!"* Burt read.

"Who did you piss off, Symone?"

"I don't know, Burt. I wish I knew. This is getting out of hand."

The station supervisor called the police and they came quickly to get the report from Symone and take the box that contained a severed head of a chicken. Whoever cut it left enough blood to spook Symone. Someone said that they were going to call Keyon to have him come pick her up. She told them not to do that and she made the call herself.

"Baby, I need you. Can you please come get me from the station? I drove, but I'm too shaken up to drive."

"I'm on my way. Be there in fifteen minutes."

Donnie smiled all the way up Peachtree Street to the radio station. She knew that if she waited patiently, played her cards right as the sympathetic, concerned friend, that one day, Symone would come to see that she needed her. Just like she had tonight. Donnie was grateful for whatever caused her lady friend distress, and thanked her lucky stars that she was the chosen one.

When she pulled up in front of the building, she saw Symone standing inside, through the glass doors, next to a heavy set white man. She got out of the car and walked up to the door so that she could escort her friend to the car. As soon as she got within a few feet, Symone came running out to her and threw her arms around her neck and cried.

"Baby, you have no idea how happy I am to see you. Something terrible happened."

"Tell me all about it, love. Let's get in the car and we can talk there."

Symone thanked the security guard for waiting with her and walked to the car with Donnie. Inside, she let the dam burst, and all her bottled up emotions of the days and the weeks that she held in, came rushing out. Donnie held her while the cried until the sobbing stopped.

"You want me to take you home now?"

"No, I can't face Keyon right now. I just want to be with you. Is that okay?"

"Your wish is my command. Let me take you to my place. I will fix you a drink and we can talk some more there. Cool?"

"Indeed it is."

The couple drove in silence until they reached Donnie's house. It never crossed Donnie's mind that Charmaine had anything to do with this because she had told Char not to fuck with Symone. And if Charmaine was nothing else, she was obedient. Symone's face was tear stained and she was still shaken up when Donnie went around to the passenger side and helped her out. The floodlight came on over the garage, lighting the sidewalk to the front door. Cool air welcomed them when Donnie opened the door.

"Come on, baby. Let's go in." Donnie prodded. Symone didn't move. In one swoop, Donnie lifted her up and carried her over the threshold to her bedroom and laid her down. She reached over her and turned on the lamp on the bedside table.

"I know you're scared, Symone. But I want you to know that I'm here for you. I ain't going nowhere. You can depend on me. You hear me, love? I got you." With that, Donnie got up and went into the kitchen and warmed a glass of milk for her friend to drink. She knew it was something she loved. By the time she got back into the room, Symone had sat up and swung her legs to the side of the bed and removed her shoes. She glanced at her watch and saw that it was almost midnight. Keyon would be worried about her but she wasn't going to call him, not right now anyway. He wouldn't do anything but try to convince her to come home and his house just didn't feel like home anymore. But being here, sitting in Donnie's bed, did.

"Hey you. How you feeling?"

Honestly? Kinda weirded out. Who would send me something like that? This shit is unreal."

"Shhh, don't cry. I'm here for you. I will protect you."

"I know. That's why I called you."

"You never have to have a reason to call me. I will always answer for you."

"I believe that."

"It's the truth. Now, lie down so you can rest and clear your weary mind."

Donnie got up and went to the hall closet, grabbed a blanket, and covered Symone up with it. She took off her own shoes and slid in bed behind her, positioning the woman's head on her arm and rocked her until she fell asleep. Donnie stared up at the ceiling and thanked the powers that be for making all her dreams come true in one night.

• • • • • • • • • • • • • • • • •

*I don't care what you do but don't you lay a hand on Symone.* As Charmaine looked at the monitor and stared at Donnie holding Symone, that's all she could think about was Donnie's parting words. It was clear that Donnie cared about Symone way more than Charmaine thought and that hurt. But Symone was not above her vengeance. Donnie said don't lay a hand on her. That left the playing field wide open for her to do whatever else she needed to do. *These bitches gon' get enough of fucking with me,* she thought, zeroing in on another monitor she had just recently set up. One by one, they would all have their day in Charmaine's court. Some sooner than others. Charmaine picked up her cell phone and sent Donnie a text.

"*Baby, I'm so sorry. Please forgive me.*" She saw Donnie's phone light up when the text came through. Donnie didn't move. Ten minutes past but it felt like an hour.

"*Did u get my last text babe? U know how much I love u. I'm nuttin' w/o u Donnie. Plz ttm....I don't care about the other girls..ur all I care about.*" No response.

"*Plz baby. Don't do me like this. Plz. I'm beggin' u.*"

This time Donnie rolled over when she realized her phone wasn't going to stop vibrating. Charmaine thought she was going to turn the phone off without replying but Donnie surprised her.

*"I know u love me. Ur ass can't help but do fucked up shit. But it's all good. U can make it up to me later. Don't text back. I'm chillin' with my brother n shit."*

Charmaine was so happy that Donnie text her back that she forgave the lie she told. She rolled over on her pallet and turned up the volume on the microphone hidden in Donnie's Ipod docking station.

"Who was that baby?" she heard Symone ask Donnie.

"Nobody important. You're all that matters," Donnie said. Symone smiled. But Charmaine cried.

Then anger followed.

• • • • • • • • • • • • • • • • •

Across town, another one of Donnie's paramours was just getting off of work. Lynn Shaw was another wannabe video vixen who had made a living using what she had to get what she wanted. She knew that one day her looks would fade, but until that happened she was stacking dollars and possessions by the truckload. Her house was dark when she walked inside. *I could have sworn I left the light on over the stove.* She walked around the house and everything seemed to be in order so she went to her bathroom and applied Noxema to her face. Then she went and plopped down on the bed and hit the power button on her TV remote. When it didn't come on, she got up to see what was going on and saw that it was unplugged. She grabbed the plug to hook it into the wall and the cord came off in her hand.

"What in the hell!" The cord had been cut off.

She checked every electronic device to find that all of them had suffered similar fates.

"I ain't even trippin'. I'm about to get paid and file and insurance claim on this shit," she said heading over to her armoire to get her camera.

When she got it off of the top shelf a sweater fell down.

Only after she tried to hang it up did she realize that one arm was cut off. She ransacked her closets and drawers and could not believe that everything she had had been destroyed. Even her shoes. She called the cops and when they arrived she showed them what was going on. A young black officer stared at her strangely when she realized she still had face cream on.

"I'm sorry. Let me go wash this off." She left the officers in the living room and rinsed her face with warm water. She picked up her facial mist and sprayed her face and immediately felt burning. She let out a blood curdling scream and the police ran in the bathroom to see what happened. They both gasped in disbelief. One called for an ambulance immediately.

"Oh my God what's happening to me?" she yelled.

"Hold still Ma'am. What did you put on your skin?"

"I sprayed a refreshing mist. I use it every night."

"Jesus. Cannon, grab that bottle for me."

The other officer picked it up and a droplet of liquid got on his finger, burning it to the bone in the process.

"Mutherfucker. It burned me. This is acid!"

They immediately took Lynn to the kitchen after carefully removing all clothing with acid on it and stood her in front of the sink, using the sprayer to flush her skin. By the time she made it to the hospital, her face was completely disfigured.

• • • • • • • • • • • • • • • • •

Keyon blew up Symone's phone. The security guard from the radio station had phoned him hours ago and saying that she had received a severed chicken head in a box. He was worried about his fiancé, and couldn't for the life of him, figure out where the hell she was. *I still have a few weeks to pay. Did they send her a chicken head to send me a message?* Thoughts like this clouded his mind. Jynx called him after she came back from her date. When he asked her if she had spoken to Symone, she sounded surprised that she wasn't at home. Neither Devine nor Cha-Cha had seen or heard from her either. None of them knew about the chicken head incident. Keyon wasn't going to tell them either. The less anyone knew the better. It was obvious that Symone was in danger and he was the reason. Guilt settled in his stomach like a brick. All he could do was pray that wherever she was, she was okay.

Symone sauntered in the house around nine the next morning. She really hated leaving Donnie's side but knew that Keyon was home waiting for her. Last night, Donnie held her in her arms and rocked her to sleep, caressing her hair, telling her that it was going to be alright. That blew her mind. She knew Donnie was feeling her in *that* way, but she kept her feelings at bay in order to give Symone what she needed, a friend. That was the difference between men and women, she thought. Women understood the needs of other women. They treated them with more respect and more tenderness than any man was capable of doing. She loved the soft hardness of Donnie's body next to hers. Her imagination ran wild thinking about what the other woman could do to turn her on. In a daze, she ran into the vase that was sitting on the pedestal in the hallway.

She caught it just in time. "Whew, that was close."

When Keyon saw Symone his first reaction was to go to her and hold her, thankful that she was okay. Then he got angry.

"Where the fuck have you been?"

"Key, baby. I didn't know you were awake. I thought you were asleep on the sofa."

"Sleep? My ass been up all night worried about you. Where were you, Symone? You have some explaining to do"

"Look, Keyon. I know I do, but now is not the time. I'm exhausted and just want to shower, slide on my pj's, and sleep. Can we discuss it later?"

"What? You stay out all night and don't think that you owe me an explanation as to where you have been? Who you were with?"

"Keyon, you know I was with Jynx . She is the only person that I call when I can't reach you or Devine."

"Oh, you were with Jynx last night?"

"Yes, I was. Do you have any more questions for me, Mr. Prosecutor?"

"Nah, no more questions. But I do have a statement. Until you learn how to be honest with me, the wedding is off. Now, go sleep on that."

• • • • • • • • • • • • • • • • •

Donnie woke up happy even though Symone left before she got up. A scented note was on her bedside table explaining that she had to get home so she wouldn't continue to worry her fiancé. It was cool with Donnie. She had to meet with Domynique that morning anyway. They sat in the corner of the McDonald's in Five Points off Marietta Street.

"I chose this spot because I know it's close to the bridge that you sleep under," Donnie teased.

Domynique flinched. "What do you want from me, Stone?"

"I want you to lose that fucked up attitude you have right now before I knock you the fuck out."

"I don't have an attitude. I was merely asking you a question."

"Who the fuck are you to question me? I'm calling the shots here, *Darling Nikki* and don't you forget that."

"I haven't forgotten, Stone," she said, hanging her head low.

For the next hour, Donnie briefed Domynique on what she had in mind. Domynique was smart enough to keep her thoughts and comments to herself. She did not agree with anything that that woman had planned, but felt like she had little choice in it. It didn't hurt that Donnie said if she completed the job successfully, then she would receive a $5,000 bonus. That was a lot of money to her. She was broke and hungry, but not stupid. Donnie had just made her an offer that she couldn't refuse.

# If It Ain't One Thing It's Another

The air was broken in the Zone Four Atlanta Police Precinct, again, and Kimora 'Kimmy' Bradshaw was sweating bullets. Her boss, Sergeant Keenan Blaire, sat five banker's boxes full of old and new, unfiled, unsolved, strange police reports on her desk. He was in charge of the Bizarre Crimes Division, but she was the one who really did all of the work. Their working relationship was similar to that of an attorney and his paralegal.

Kimmy had only been in the Bizarre Crimes Division for a little over two months. It had taken her that long to come up with a filing system that she could work with. Vandalisms, simple batteries, destruction of property and so on all had their own pile. Then she made a cross section according to the complainants' initial date of report and the case number.

She'd been sitting at her desk for weeks, working on the new system, and stood to stretch. She marveled at her handy work. Now, she would be able to go through each report and follow up. Sergeant Blaire walked in pushing an industrial sized fan that he plugged in and turned on full speed. The force of air blew everything that wasn't nailed down across the room. Kimmy watched all of her hard work blow away. The sergeant offered his meager apologies and helped her pick up the papers. A woman who had lost her hair, an acid victim whose clothes, face and shoes had all been destroyed; and another who found a dead cat in her car and many more victims would have to wait a little while longer for justice to be served. And the list would continue to grow.

● ● ● ● ● ● ● ● ● ● ● ● ● ● ● ● ●

Nina Carter was going to miss her flight if the car she hired didn't hurry up. Everytime she called the company, she kept getting a busy signal. Everything she'd worked so hard rested on this one meeting.

"Odessa! Get your dumbass in here!" she yelled to her housekeeper. "Where did you find this lame ass car service? Didn't I tell you how important today is to me? To us? If I don't get this promotion I'm firing your stupid ass and you can go back and stand in the welfare line."

"I don't get welfare."

"Whatever, all you people are just the same. Uneducated and willfully ignorant," Nina said haughtily.

"I'm smart enough to know that you should have left two hours ago. And I'm damned sure smart enough to know when to leave well enough alone."

"What are you talking about Odessa? You know what? Don't even bother explaining. You're fired! Get your shit and take your grocery bag carrying ass out of my house."

"You college bitches are all the same. Think because you have a degree you can say and do whatever you want. That's where your ass is wrong. But you gon' learn today," she ended, hitting the woman hard in the head with a ceramic statue, knocking her out. When Nina came to, she was bound to a chair and her housekeeper was dousing everything in her bedroom with gasoline.

"Odessa, I know I may have hurt your feelings but don't you think this is going too far? You can't do this. Let's be rational."

"You didn't hurt my feelings, you fucked my woman. This is about to go further, you know. I can and will do this. And I'm never rational."

"I didn't fuck your woman. I'm not a damn dyke. Untie

me! Now!"

"Yeah you fucked Donnie. I wasn't tripping at first. I figured it was just once, but you kept coming back for more. And you may not think your ass is a lesbo because you're a pillow princess.

"D-Donnie never told me he had a woman. I never would have messed with her. I'm sorry and I don't know what a pillow princess is."

"That's a bitch like you who loves for studs to eat your pussy, fuck you and make you cum, while you just lay there. You don't reciprocate. But it's all good. It won't happen again."

The housekeeper poured a gasoline circle around the chair and trailed it out of the door. Then she went to the kitchen, locked the windows and doors and turned on the gas stove but blew the fire out. She put a metal bowl in the microwave and then turned it on and finally, she lit a match and put it on the gas trail. Nina screamed to the top of her lungs hoping someone would hear her. No one ever did. By the time the housekeeper boarded the bus two blocks away, Nina Carter was dead.

Charmaine sat comfortably on the bus next to her willing accomplice who had just earned $25,000. It wasn't hard for Charmaine to convince the elderly lady to assist her because she hated her and Nina never failed to belittle the loyal maid daily. There was only so much one person could take. Charmaine found that out one day she followed the woman home and struck up a conversation with her. She saw smoke billow in the air and began to sing softly. "One dark night, when Donnie was in bed, old Nina Carter said baby give me some head. I tried to warn her, she dismissed me and now that bitch is dead… It's a hot time in the A-town tonight. Fire! Fire! Fire!

● ● ● ● ● ● ● ● ● ● ● ● ● ● ● ● ●

Northeast of Atlanta, in Gwinnet County, Tranice Rice was being pulled over by the police. She was extremely agitated because she didn't know why. It was common knowledge that

71

Gwinnett County was not the place to be fucked with because it was a known speed trap and they set their own price on tickets. When you go to court, if you don't have the money to pay the fine in full, they set up a payment plan and place you on probation and you have to pay the ticket plus a probation fee. Gwinnett County was something like a pimp. As she sat there in her car, waiting for the officer to get out of his cruiser, she believed it.

A look in her rear view mirror told her that something serious was going on. Not one, but two more cruisers came. One of them parked in front of her, the other right beside the driver side door. She was boxed in. The cop who pulled her over came up to her vehicle and tapped hard on the glass. She hit the automatic button and the window came down slowly.

"Why did you pull me over, Sir?"

"We'll get to that in a minute, lil' lady. License and registration please."

She gave the cop what he asked for and he walked back to his car and ran her plates. He took his sweet time coming back. The other cops had gotten out of their cars and they were in the back chatting away. All of them laughed at something one of them had said and that pissed her off even further because she didn't see anything funny about being stopped in the middle of a hot Georgia day. Ten minutes later, the cop came back and asked her to step out of the car.

"For what? I didn't do anything."

"That's what they all say. I'm going to sit you right here, while we search this vehicle. I'm not going to cuff you, but don't make me regret it."

A dog came out of nowhere and began to sniff around the car. He stopped by the right rear tire and started barking viciously.

"We got a hit, fellas," one of the officers said, leaning under the car.

"Well, well, well. Look what we have here."

Tranice saw a bag of pills, weed and some small brown

vials. "That shit ain't mine. This is a setup."

"That's something we never heard before." All the cops laughed.

"But this ain't even my car. My friend lemme drive it. You can call and ask him."

"That's why I pulled you over. A car matching this one came up in the system as stolen. The VIN number matches as well. It's registered to a known Florida drug dealer. Is that the friend you want me to call?" he finished snidely.

"I didn't do this. I didn't steal a car or have those drugs," Tranice pleaded.

"So tell me, if you didn't steal this car or have that dope, who did?"

"I have no idea."

"You're in big trouble, lil' lady. You could be facing ten or more years in prison for all this."

"What! But I'm innocent I tell you. Innocent!" she yelled.

"Yeah, that's what they all say."

"But you're not even trying to listen to my side."

"That's not my job. Tell it to the judge."

• • • • • • • • • • • • • • • • • •

That night, Charmaine called Gwinnett County jail to find that Tranice Rice was in jail with a $250, 000 bail bond. She was charged with grand theft auto and possession of a controlled dangerous substance with the intent to distribute. Unless she had a good attorney, she was fucked. Charmaine licked the seal on the envelope of the note she had just written Tranice and prepared it for the mail. *You should have listened and left Donnie alone* was all that it said. Happy, Charmaine began to sing, bobbing her head to the beat.

"*....and another one's gone and another's gone, another one bites the dust...hey, I'm gonna get you too, another one bites the dust.*" That was a promise.

# Tonight Is The Night

Labor Day weekend had started off with a bang. So many festivities were going on around the city. Ludacris was hosting his annual Luda Day weekend, college football season was kicking off and Atlanta Black Gay Pride week was about to go down. Everyone knew that Atlanta held the biggest, baddest, and best Black Pride week. People came from all over just to say that they were there.

In separate homes, Donnie, Cha-Cha and Devine all prepared to go celebrate. For Donnie, this was a breeding ground for new pussy. Although things between her and Symone were progressing smoothly, they still hadn't fucked yet. Symone had yet to allow Donnie the opportunity to taste her sweet nectar and lick the insides of her nether lips. She would wait on her because that was the woman she wanted, but she needed to get her rocks off in the meantime and what better way to do it than with new pussy?

Devine, whose current relationship status was 'it's complicated', wasn't looking for anything serious or a fling. Pride week for him was more than fellowship with others. It was also a time for self-reflection and revelation. During the Pride parade in 2005, Devin decided to come out to his family. His mother knew that her son had a little sugar in his tank yet loved him anyway. But having a gay son was a bitter pill to swallow for his dad who had always considered himself a ladies' man. He didn't quite know what to say when his youngest son revealed his sexual orientation to him. But he loved him no matter what and every year he came to Pride to support his flamingly gay baby boy.

Unfortunately for Cha-Cha, her parents did not receive the news of having a gay son so well. As the staunch Catholic family that they were, they were against it. When Cha-Cha told them that she was having the gender reassignment surgery they had called her an abomination to their faith and disowned her. She hadn't spoken to any blood relative in her family in three years. That was their choice. She had to live her life, her way. It had been less two months since her gender reassignment was complete but she looked and felt amazing. She was officially a woman.

· · · · · · · · · · · · · · · · ·

In Buckhead, Keyon was making preparations as well. Today was the M.O.S. Anniversary Party and D-day. He would finally be able to pay off the debt that he'd kept secret from everyone, and had been bringing havoc on his life. Only $5 million left to go and the $25 million dollar debt would be paid. He let out a huge sigh of relief as he groomed himself in front of the mirror, and thought about the first five years in business, and how he'd gotten himself in so much trouble. Keyon had applied for loans at over twenty banks and had been turned down by all of them. One of Keyon's frat brother's had told him about an investment banker who specialized in small business lending.

He'd already started Man of Steele records but it was just a small label. Keyon knew with the right amount of capital, he could run with the big dogs. The talent show they'd hosted had brought out some of the city's hottest talent and they were all hungry and ready to hustle. He knew that with the right backing, many of them could be Grammy award winning artists. All he needed was someone to give him a chance.

When Keyon walked into the bank he had his speech prepared and his presentation. He walked over to the reception-ist and told her that he was there for a two o'clock appointment with the president. She placed a call announcing that he had arrived and then ushered him into the office.

"Mr. Abignol will be with you in a moment."

Keyon tapped his foot rapidly as he waited for the man to join him.

"Nervous? Don't be. We make lending easy here at Surety Bank and Trust, Mr. Steele," the man said as he walked over.

The gentleman shook his hand warmly and told him to have a seat after Keyon stood to greet him. The two made small talk to break the ice. While the other man talked, Keyon sized him up. Mr. Abignol was about five feet seven inches with a dark brown complexion. His nose was wide and his lips were full, like Lionel Richie's. His neck was thick and virtually non-existent. It looked like someone had pushed his head into his shoulders, like Keyon's girl cousins used to do with their dolls. Keyon couldn't help but wonder how much play this man got with women because he was so weird looking. He wore these wire-rimmed glasses that made his eyes look beady and he had lots of razor bumps on his chin and neck.

"Now, let's get down to business. But first, call me Big. All of my friends do. No need for too many formalities."

"Okay, thank you," Keyon replied and began to lay out his presentation meticulously. Mr. Abignol seemed impressed by the numbers that Keyon laid out to him and looked like he was genuinely interest in helping him.

"How much are you asking for at this time?" the banker asked.

Keyon hesitated, "Um, five million?" He really needed more, but was scared to put the larger number out there, afraid of being turned down again.

"Is that realistic? I mean, music videos alone can run into the millions depending on how lavish they are and then what about payroll? How many people are currently on your staff?"

Keyon answered all of the man's questions and then they reviewed the numbers again. Mr. Abignol then pulled out a calculator and note pad and rolled up his sleeves. No other banker had gotten this involved in his presentation so Keyon took that as a good sign.

"Everything sounds real good," Mr. Abignol began. "For what you're trying to accomplish though, you are going to need a minimum of $25,000,000 not the five that you're asking."

"Yes, Sir. Initially, I was requesting more but after meeting with the other lenders and being turned down, I reduced the amount. I figured if someone was willing to loan me the five million and I got that paid off, they would not have a problem if I came back again asking for more."

"I see. Well, like I said. It all sounds good and the music industry is booming right now. Unfortunately, the most the bank would be able to loan you at this time is one million dollars. It's too risky to invest that much money into a business that we don't know will succeed or not."

Deflated, Keyon stood and prepared to leave. "I understand, Sir. Thank you so much for your time."

"Now wait a minute. I said the bank can't loan you the money, but I didn't say that I couldn't."

"I'm not following you." Keyon said confused.

"I have another company Big Loans, Underwriting and Development and we would love to be in bed with you. So this is what I'm prepared to do. I will loan you the $25 million dollars at 15% interest to be paid off in five years. Your first payment will be eight million dollars, due one year after we sign on the dotted line. That way, you can break your payments up into equal increments. After that, you can make monthly payments or annually, I like choices so I will let you decide on that. It doesn't matter as long as I get paid at least seven million dollars by year's end."

"Twenty-five mil is a lot of money."

"I know it. But you just laid out a business plan worth three times. Are you saying you can't pull it off?"

"Not at all. I know me and my team can get it done," Keyon replied.

"So, do we have a deal?"

"Yes we do." Two weeks later, Keyon and his new friend Big signed the contract and Keyon had the money he needed. He moved Man of Steele Records into the Equifax building in downtown Atlanta and they began to hustle.

Yes, he and his staff had experienced a lot. But through it all, it was worth it; especially his humble beginnings, which was how he met Symone. From the first time he laid eyes on her Keyon knew that he wanted to make her his wife. She was such a beautiful, intelligent woman and she didn't fawn over him because of who he was. He could be himself around her and felt comfortable sharing his hopes, dreams and even fears with her. They started off so strong. Their love was hotter than a three-alarm fire. Now, the spark barely kindled. Two goal-oriented and driven people could be together and have a successful, love filled relationship *if* they wanted that. It would take work on both of their parts, but it was possible. He was willing to do whatever it took to make their relationship work. The problem was she wasn't.

Keyon stepped away from the mirror and thought about the fact that they still hadn't had the 'talk', and it appeared to him that she was avoiding it at all costs. He knew that she continued to talk online to this Don Juan character and had a sneaking suspicion that the two of them had done a little more than just talk. Sometimes, he wished he had a woman's intuition. Keyon was not unrealistic. He knew that Symone might not be the woman that God intended for him. She was certainly doing everything in her power to prove him right on that fact. He knew there was a woman out there who would love him and want to be with him in return even if Symone didn't. He just had to find her.

● ● ● ● ● ● ● ● ● ● ● ● ● ● ● ● ●

The Glam Spot Salon buzzed with activity. It was one of Atlanta's premiere full service salon's that catered to the rich and famous and also the not-so-rich and not-so-famous. Jynx had been getting her hair done by Salina Hill, the salon owner, since they were in junior high. Jynx was the first person to sit in her styling chair when she opened the shop; the same chair that she was sitting in now.

Symone had been getting her hair done there for five years. Being with Keyon definitely had its perks because this place was pricey. Although she was making pretty good money at the radio station, Symone was sure that she could have found a decent salon that didn't cost nearly as much as this one. But Keyon spared no expense when it came to her, financially, physically or emotionally. He always gave her the very best. Today, he had paid for both her and Jynx to have the works. He said that when they walked into the hotel that evening, that they would be the envy of every woman there.

"*I want to show you off babe,*" he told Symone when they were still speaking. Or rather when she was still speaking to him. He arranged for them to get their hair, nails and make up done before being chauffeured to Michael E. Knights, where they would be fitted in their custom made, and one-of-a-kind dresses.

For any other woman, this would all be great. But Symone was over all of it. All this preparation for what? Truth be told, Symone didn't even want to go. If she had it her way, she and Donnie would go to the movies or dinner or something. Anything. It didn't even matter to her, as long as they were together. She was beginning to depend on the times they spoke and saw one another. Donnie always knew the right things to say, the right things to do, to make her feel better. Her thoughts must have shown on her face because Jynx chimed in and asked her what was wrong.

"Nothing. I was just thinking about tonight. I know it's gonna be so many people there. You know how I feel about large crowds."

"Girl, you don't mind crowds and you know it. Come clean, Symone. What's really going on? You have been a bit standoffish lately and I wanna know why."

"Look, Jynx. I just have a lot going on right now and I don't wanna sound mean, but I just don't want to talk about it."

"I realize that things between you and Keyon have been a bit strained lately, but talking about it will help you work through any issues you may have."

"Will you please stop trying to psycho-analyze me? I'm not one of your patients. Excuse me, *clients*. Whatever you call them. I already told you I don't want to talk about it!" Symone snapped.

"You know what? For the past few weeks you have been on some other shit. Accusing my cousin of cheating. Accusing me of Lord knows what because *you* forgot your own man's birthday. It's been unreal. And up until now, both Devine and I have been holding our tongues. But this bullshit right here is for the birds. I have tried to be nothing but a friend to you since you have dated my cousin. I tried to show you that your relationship with him has nothing to do with the friendship you and I have. Keyon's a good man. He really loves you. Most women would kill to have a man treat them half as well as he does you. But the bottom line is that no matter what anyone does for you, your ass is *never* satisfied."

"If I hear how good of a man Keyon is or how lucky I am to be with him one more time I swear I'm going to throw up. His shit stinks just like everyone else's and he ain't perfect. Just because he is rich and handsome does not make him the ultimate catch. There are other things that make up a relationship than just sex and money. Hell, you all are always talking about shit he's done like I didn't help him with any of it. What about all the sacrifices that I made? I gave up a lot to be with him. Put my goals on hold so he could reach his. He wouldn't be where he is today if it wasn't for me."

"You? What the hell have you done? M.O.S. was already established by the time you came into the picture. My cousin poured every dime he had and even some he didn't into that company. I was there watching him live in a one bedroom apartment on Bankhead, eating noodles and drinking water so he could save. He wouldn't even take money from anyone in the family because if this company didn't take off, he didn't want anyone to suffer a loss."

"Yes, I admit, M.O.S. saw a huge breakthrough in the young adult market when your brother's group signed on. But it was Keyon's genius that took them from mere talent show contestants to triple platinum artists. As I recall, the only thing you have ever done to help Keyon or his company is talk it up on your show. While I'm sure he appreciates the free publicity that you give him, his accomplishments are just that. His. You really need to get over yourself."

"Ugh, Donnie told me that this would happen."

"That what would happen?"

"That you all would turn on me. I see what this is and I don't have to sit around and listen to this anymore. I'm outta here. F-Y-I, I've been very satisfied lately, just not by Keyon."

The salon was quiet with the exception of the hum of the dryer and running water. Jynx had forgotten where they were. All eyes were on her. Even Salina stood, quietly, staring at her. Embarrassed, she slumped down in her chair and raised the magazine to cover her face. Things happen. Friends argue. This was nothing new. Soon, the conversations had started back up and no one thought twice about what just happened.

No one but Jynx.

• • • • • • • • • • • • • • • • •

"*It's going down tonight, tonight is goes down. It's going down tonight. Tonight it's gonna go down,*" Donnie sang.

Celly Cel didn't know how right he was. She waited so patiently for this and in a few short hours, everything that she wanted would finally be hers.

"Domynique, pay attention! I don't need you fucking this up for me. Are we clear on what your role is? Do I need to go over it again?"

"No. I'm clear."

"Where the hell is your wig?"

"It's in my bag. But why do I have to wear a wig again?" Her question was met with a hard slap across her right cheek.

"Stop questioning me! I swear your ass is gonna make me fuck you up before all of this is over. Just do what the fuck I say, bitch!" Donnie shouted. Now, you are NOT to leave out of this room. Do you hear me?"

"Yes."

"I already have the cameras and sound equipment in place. I gotta go. The guests are starting to arrive. Remember, if you pull this off, there's five grand in it for you."

Donnie smacked the other woman's ass and left out of the suite.

● ● ● ● ● ● ● ● ● ● ● ● ● ● ● ● ●

"How long will you be staying with us, Mrs. Wimberley?" the front desk agent asked.

"Oh, just for two days. My son's family will be meeting me here tomorrow and the next day we will be flying to Paris. My grandkids are getting so big. I can't wait to see them again."

"How many do you have?"

"Four," the elderly woman answered, pulling out pictures of the children.

"Wow, these are some beautiful children. They should think about modeling. They definitely would have a career in it."

"I get that all the time, dear. But they are too cantankerous to sit still long enough for a cameraman. It took three hours just to get these shots."

The desk clerk laughed and finished checking the woman in. "Here is your key card. Your suite number is 1471. Gavin will help you up with your bags. If there is anything that you need just dial '0' on your phone in the room and it will ring the desk. We will take care of all of your needs."

"Thank you so much. You all are so friendly here."

"You're welcome, Mrs. Wimberley. Enjoy your stay at the W Perimeter."

The old lady dismissed the bellhop. She did not need help with her bags. They weren't heavy and she wasn't weak. She stepped onto the elevator with a young couple who was in love. They necked and snuggled all the way to the fourth floor where they got off.

"If they hadn't already, I was about to tell them to get a room. Geesh." Before exiting on the 14th floor, she took her glasses off and turned them around, lenses facing her. "This is going to be a very interesting night. Watch what happens next."

# Lights. Camera. Action...

Glamorous people milled around the grand ballroom of the hotel. The music pumped, the room had beautiful décor, and there was food and drinks galore. Conversations flowed as freely as the liquor. An open bar may not have been such a good idea, but most of the partygoers were either staying at the hotel or one nearby. Over the next couple of hours, the party would kick into overdrive.

Keyon spoke to Jynx while she was still at the salon so he knew what happened, but he didn't understand why Symone wasn't with him. *This must be her way of paying me back for missing her big night a few months ago,* he thought. Symone had changed. She was not the woman he met and fell in love with. Right now, she wasn't even a woman that he liked. Jynx didn't leave out any details when she relayed the story to him. Not sparing his feelings, she told him that Symone said she was very satisfied, just not by him. That implied that she fucked someone else. That would explain why the two of them had not had sex in months. His sexual interactions lately had been limited to him jacking off in the shower.

"Are you having a good time?" Judy asked, interrupting his thoughts.

"Yeah. It's cool."

"Well, then wipe that scowl off your face. You look like you're going to punch someone in the face if they come too close to you."

"I hadn't realized. My bad."

"I noticed Symone didn't show up. Things still tense at home?"

"You don't know the half of it, J."

"Well, I know that tonight is supposed to be a celebration, but tomorrow, why don't you come over and have Sunday dinner with me and my family? You know Shawn would love to have you over. Plus, Mother will be there too, and you know how she digs you."

"Judy, you're the only woman I know who keeps trying to fix me up with her 85 year old mother."

"Hell, Liza is hot. She's been around the block a few times but I'm sure with her experience she will teach you a few things."

"Funny. Let's get a drink and some food. It's almost time for my speech and you know how much I hate those."

"Yes, I do. That's why I have arranged for someone else to speak first. All you will have to do is say 'Thank you all for coming. God bless you. Good night.'"

"You're a hot mess."

Keyon told Judy he had to run to the bathroom and she made her way to the podium. She tapped on the microphone and got the crowd's attention and spoke a bit to stall and give Keyon time to get back. After opening with a few lame jokes, she introduced the special guest of the evening.

"I know none of you were expecting to see this young man seeing as how he and his group SKY-Hi have been on tour in Europe." Applause broke out around the room and she had to wait until it died down before she continued. "But they have decided to take a break and grace us with their presence, if only for one night, to help celebrate the man who we have all come to love and sometimes, like, our boss, Keyon Steele. Ladies and Gentlemen, Shymon Morrow." More applause rang out as the young man took the stage.

"Hey everybody. Me and the guys couldn't miss tonight. If it weren't for Keyon putting us on M.O.S., there would be no tour right now. He helped make all of our dreams come true. Before we got our record deal, we thought all we had to do was sing and get paid. But Keyon took us in and taught us the business side of music. We are proud of you, man. Who would have thought that five years ago, when I walked into the civic center that we would be standing here today, sharing a moment like this? All of your artists dropped what we were doing to come and celebrate your night with you. That should tell all of you what kind of man this is. None of us…" He pointed across the room, "…would be here tonight if this man would have given up when things got tough. None of us would be eating as well as we are today. Thank you, Keyon. And congratulations. I love you brother-in-law. Now everyone raise your glass and help me toast the man of the hour, Keyon Steele."

"Salute!" Glasses clinked for the toast. Everyone looked around for him, expecting him to come onstage but he didn't. Little did everyone know, Keyon was handling overdue business outside.

"Looks like you've missed your cue," the man said.

"What's this about? I gave Big the money."

"Yeah, I know. I counted it."

"Then what's the problem?"

"I came here to give you this," he said, punching Keyon hard in his stomach, three times. Keyon sputtered as he slid to the floor. "That's a sincere congratulatory love tap from Big. By the way, expect another call. The Boss ain't through with you yet. Or that pretty little fiancé of yours."

"Stay away from Symone or else…"

"Or else, what? Nigga, you ain't in no position to be threatening nobody. I suggest you fall in line or your Mama will be mourning her only son." He gave Keyon a look that ceased all conversation and he walked out of the restroom.

Coughing, Keyon rolled up on his knees and looked at his disheveled appearance in the mirror. He hurried up and washed his face and fixed his clothes before exiting. The crowd began to chant his name. Keyon stepped out of the bathroom and walked the narrow hallway continuing to hear the chanting of his name. He walked up to the microphone looking calm and composed, but inside he was scared as hell. What had he gotten himself into and how would he ever get out?

"Judy said I wouldn't have to say much so I'm going to keep this short and sweet. The only reason I didn't give up was because God wouldn't let me. I knew that M.O.S. could be great. We are growing by leaps and bounds and it is because of the hard work and dedication of all of you. You're the best team a man could ask for. I couldn't do it alone. I'm so blessed that I don't have to. Here's to five more years!" He raised his glass then drank.

With all the formalities out of the way, the party resumed. They danced, drank and were very merry.

"A fresh drink, sir?" the bartender asked Keyon.

"Sure. Gimme a shot of Patron."

"Patron? You don't look like a Patron man to me. I've been working on a new drink. I like to call it The Man of Steele"

"Word, dude? You named a drink after the company? That's some cool shit right there."

"Yeah. I'm known for customizing drinks for my high profile clients. They like that exclusivity. Here, try this. Tell me what you think."

Keyon drank the dark liquor that tasted like a very fine Cognac mixed with a little Rum. It was smooth going down.

"I like that. Serve that to the other guests, please," Keyon said, getting ready to walk off. "And if I don't make it back over here tonight, make sure my assistant Judy gets your card. I'd like to use your services at other M.O.S. events."

"That's what's up. I'll do that." *Enjoy your drink, motherfucker.* Donnie was quite pleased with her handy work. It wouldn't be long now. She rubbed her hands together and licked her lips. Her work was done here. It was time to go upstairs.

•  •  •  •  •  •  •  •  •  •  •  •  •  •  •  •  •

Around one a.m. Keyon began to feel a bit woozy. He

needed to sit down.

"May I help you, sir? You look a bit tipsy," a pretty Latino woman asked.

"Yeah. I guess I had too much to drink. I don't usually drink this much."

"The hotel has prepared a complimentary suite for you. If you'll allow me, I can escort you there. You can rest for a bit and come back and join the party later. It doesn't look like anyone is leaving anytime soon."

"Man, you guys give great service. Lead the way." That was the last thing Keyon would remember.

The young lady took him to room 1470. Once inside, he began to stagger. He leaned his full 200 plus pounds on her small five-two, 110-pound frame.

"Help me with this motherfucker. Don't just stand there," she pleaded. Donnie came out of the shadows and helped her walk him to the bed. They made quick work of stripping him out of his shoes and then clothing. He was so out of it.

"Symone, I knew you would come," he said. "I love you, girl." Donnie punched him in the head when he said that. Keyon was too zonked to feel it.

"What the hell did you do that for?" Angel asked, puzzled.

"No reason. Pull the covers back and set the lighting. Domynique, are you ready?"

Domynique came out of the bathroom, naked, with the exception of the short red wig that she wore. Donnie gawked at the sight. Even Angel had to stop to admire the woman's beautiful body.

"Damn, Stone. You sure know how to pick 'em, don't chu?"

"Hell, yeah. Alright, come on over here and work your magic. Angel, you can head on home. I'll be there in a few. I just gotta wrap up some loose ends here." She kissed her Latina paramour and walked her to the door, locking it behind her after she left out.

Domynique climbed in bed with Keyon. He was such a beautiful sight to behold; fine chiseled features, washboard abs, long, lean, muscular legs, and kissable lips.

"What the fuck you waiting on? I ain't got all night. Do what I told you and you won't go wrong."

Domynique leaned over the drugged man and kissed his lips. They were even softer than they looked. She outlined his lips with her tongue and then slipped it inside. Stone had told her that he might respond. He returned her kiss and pulled her into him. His hands traveled the length of her body and she felt her center get wet with need. She kissed down his neck and licked slowly around his nipples, gently biting each one. Hands moved down until she came in contact with his hard dick. Her little hands massaged and stroked him and then her mouth was where her hands once were. With long slow strokes of her tongue, she sucked him into further oblivion.

Before she knew what was happening, he pulled her up and turned her over on her back and began to lick her pussy with such force that she cried out. He suckled on her clitoris and penetrated her with his fingers at the same damn time. Never, in all her 26 years of living had she ever felt like this. Her hips gyrated, as he loved on her with his mouth. Her legs shook violently as her cum poured down his throat. A delirious Keyon moved upwards and sucked her breast. He gave each one equal attention, teasing her, pleasing her with each flick of his tongue. Domynique felt the tip of his dick at her opening and braced herself for the unknown. He rubbed it up and down over her moist clit, wetting the head, before plunging in to the hilt, breaking the thin barrier that officially made her a woman. A burning sensation overtook Domynique and a tear slid down her face. Keyon, unaware of what was really going on, began a slow, steady dance with their bodies, allowing her to adjust to his size and the newness of it all.

They continued in the missionary position until Keyon rolled over and brought her with him. She was positioned over his meat and slid down slowly, taking him all in. Because her legs were bent on either side of him, she used them to help her rise and fall to pleasure him. Domynique, who had been too busy trying to survive, was probably one of the few people in the world who did not know who Keyon Steele was. Looking down at him, she began to imagine what life would be like if this fine specimen of a man was hers. But a girl like her could never be so lucky. No man in his right mind would be interested in her. She had come from nothing and recent events as of late would ensure that she would never have anything either. Again, a tear fell down her cheek but this time, a few more.

The pace of their lovemaking increased and Keyon grabbed hold of Domynique's hips and drove home inside her. He rammed his dick in her with power and finesse. A low growl started in his throat and escaped through his lips as he came, spilling his seed inside her. Domynique collapsed on his chest, exhausted. *I have got to do this again. What the hell was I waiting for?* She thought. His arms snaked up around her and held her close to him. She had never been held like that. She probably wouldn't ever be again so she made herself at home in his arms. A few minutes later, she heard snoring. Then Stone's voice, breaking the romantic mood she had set for herself.

"That was some good shit, Darling Nikki. Now I see why they call your ass that. My dick got hard watching you get his dick sloppy wet. You sucked the shit outta that piece. If I had known that you could do it like that, I would have let you slob on my knob. I still might."

"You don't have a kn…" she began before catching herself.

Donnie looked at her with fury in her eyes and walked over to her and punched her in the stomach. Domynique leaned over in pain and then Donnie slapped her face. The other woman tried to run away, but was caught by her long hair after the wig fell off and pulled back into a fist. Donnie beat her for the next few minutes. Punishing her for the reminder that she didn't have a real penis like she wanted. She kicked Domynique while she was down on the floor and spit on her naked form.

"That's what your ass gets. You'll know better next time, won't you? Get your ass up and help me pack this shit up. We gotta go."

Thirty minutes later, all of the equipment was packed up and Domynique was dressed. The lampshades that had been removed to provide maximum light had been put back onto the lamps. All surfaces had been wiped clean. Donnie didn't want any traces of her there at the hotel. Domynique walked over to the bed and covered Keyon up. She wanted so badly to kiss him goodbye. But she knew that Donnie would hit her again if she tried it. Instead, she turned off the lamp and exited the room.

● ● ● ● ● ● ● ● ● ● ● ● ● ● ● ● ● ●

Charmaine pulled the wire camera from under the adjoining door. She couldn't believe what she'd just taped. *I knew Donnie was up to something, but I never imagined this.* She set up her laptop so that she could review the footage. This was definitely too good to be true. Charmaine knew she would be able to use this to her advantage. After watching the tape twice and masturbating, she fell asleep and let the softness of the five-star hotel's comfortable blanket envelope her.

● ● ● ● ● ● ● ● ● ● ● ● ● ● ● ● ● ●

Keyon woke up drained in more ways than one. His head was still spinning a bit when he sat up in the bed. He shook his head trying to shake the fuzziness out. The last thing he remembered was drinking and dancing with Malia, the lead singer of one of his girl groups. A bartender had made him a signature drink and then this Mexican chick appeared out of nowhere. What happened after that was beyond him. He threw the covers back and immediately yelled out "What the fuck is this?" There was blood smeared on the sheets and on his dick. A lot of it. *"What the hell have I done?"*

Nervously, he got up and gathered up the bloody sheets. He stuffed them inside one of the plastic laundry bags that he found in the armoire and quickly dressed. Those sheets were coming with him. He would send the hotel a check to cover the cost. His body told him that he had had sex last night and busted a nut, a few of them. The sheets told him that she had been a virgin, he hoped. He didn't want to think about where the blood came from if she hadn't been one. *I'm never going to drink again. This is some weird shit,* he thought.

And it was about to get weirder.

AveryGOODE

# Sex, Lies and Videotape

A drunk ain't shit, and now Keyon knew why. His head still spun even though the party was two days ago. How he managed to get through dinner at Judy's house yesterday he didn't know. But he promised himself, that if he ever drank again, it would not be anything more than one glass of champagne. He rested his head in his hands and exhaled loudly. Things at home hadn't improved. Symone lied to Keyon and told him that the reason she didn't show at his anniversary party was because she was on the phone consoling her brother, who was thousands of miles away. She had no idea he'd flown in town for the party.

"So, you were on the phone with Shymon the whole night?"

"Yes, I was. He was upset that our parents weren't around to see him perform in London for the Queen. The freakin' Queen of England! Who knew she was a fan of SKY-Hi?"

"Stop, Symone."

"I mean, baby brother is really doing big things now, isn't he? I'm so proud of him. So yeah, I sat up on the phone with him and we talked about our parents. We really miss them."

"I said STOP, Symone! Stop all this lying. I don't know what the hell you were doing last night but I know for damned sure you weren't talking to your brother. Shymon, Khalif and Yancy were all at the party last night. Yeah, that's right. So close your damn mouth, because you're busted."

"He came in last night? He was there?" she asked.

"Damn, you just don't get it do you? I love you, Symone, with everything I have in me. Your lying is pushing me away. Our wedding is already postponed because of it. I'm busting my ass to make you happy. What more do you want from me?

"Well for starters, I want you to be honest with me. How did you get into that accident? And why when I come into the room you hurry up and end conversations? Are you cheating on me? What's really going on with you, Keyon, because it's affecting us?"

"I'm not cheating on you and my accident was just that, an accident. There's nothing going on with me other than business, I assure you."

"And you call me a liar. This some bullshit, Keyon. I guess whenever you're willing to tell me the truth that's when I will come clean, too. Until then..." her voice trailed off

"Until then, Symone? Make it clear."

"Until then, I'm going to breakfast with a friend and I don't want to talk about this anymore. Peace." She threw up two fingers, swung her handbag over her shoulder and prepared to leave.

"Symone, wait. Don't go! It's not safe for you to leave right now." Keyon realized too late that he had said too much.

"Not safe? And why is that, Keyon?"

He hesitated answering, looking for the right thing to say without telling her the truth. "You shouldn't drive when you are upset. You're not as focused. Please, just stay here and let's work this out. I love you," he said, trying to close the can of worms he just opened.

Symone laughed at his explanation and said "well, we all gotta go sometime" and walked out of the door.

●●●●●●●●●●●●●●●●●●

When she made it back in that night, Keyon heard her creep past the guest bedroom. The door was ajar and he saw her shadow in the moonlight. He loved Symone and was glad that she was safe and he would do all that he could to make sure that she stayed that way. But Symone was really frustrating him and if Big didn't kill her, he just might.

He was still trying to sort through the events of Friday night. When he was at Judy's house yesterday, he questioned her on what she had seen. But she wasn't much help. Judy and her husband Shawn left the party a little before midnight. It was too embarrassing to admit that he was so out of it he couldn't remember, so he played it cool. Shawn told him that from the looks of it, everyone was having a great time. Keyon decided to do some work, instead of dwelling on the past. *Eventually, I will figure it out.*

Judy came in and dropped the daily mail off on his desk and gave him his agenda. The two of them worked steadily until five, at which time, Judy got up to leave for the day. Keyon went to the studio to see what was happening. A new group was working on their first CD. The six members, who were made of three men and three women, played their own instruments and sang from the soul. They were also siblings. One of the producers had a great idea for them to remake an older R&B song. They chose a song by the group SKYY, *Real Love.* Keyon sat back and listened to Ali, the youngest sister, belt out the soulful lyrics.

*I know it's not the first time,*
*That you've ever felt this way before,*
*Ooh, but those memories are still lasting,*
*Of the pain you got for your trusting,*
*So when love calls you walk out the door,*
*Oh, but this time boy,*
*Don't be afraid of the way you feel,*
*Open your heart and you'll see it's real,*
*It's real love.*

Ali sang the song with such passion as if she penned it. She sang like she knew the pain of begging someone to open his heart to let her in. Let her love him like he deserved to be. Not to punish her for someone else's mistakes. Keyon understood the songwriter's pleas. He had been making them himself. All he wanted was for things to be right between him and his lady love and he was going to do whatever it took to make sure they were.

He sat in the studio a little while longer. Offering a suggestion here and there when needed and then decided to call it a day. He took the elevator back up to his office and saw that night had fallen over the city. Atlanta was beautiful at night. There was 180 degrees of glass in his 27th floor office that offered some of the best views in town. Man of Steele Records occupied five floors of a high-rise office complex in midtown Atlanta, and even though he was not on the top floor, he could still appreciate the view from here.

The mail Judy had placed on his desk still sat there. He grabbed a bottle of water out of the mini-fridge and began to go through each piece. Judy highlighted the key points in a few pieces of correspondence that he needed to pay attention to. Some things only required his signature, while some of the mail required no action at all on his part. There was a small package that was addressed to him and marked 'Congratulations' that Judy didn't open. Keyon grabbed his letter opener and pulled the CD case out. Mistakenly, he thought it was a demo. He put it in the CD player but nothing happened. After further examination, he realized it was a DVD. He put it in the DVD player and pressed play. His back was only turned for a few seconds but the volume on his TV was loud enough for him to hear the familiar sounds of sex.

He abruptly turned around to see one of the most beautiful women he'd seen in a long time being pleasured by him. Even her fuck faces were beautiful. Her small hands held his head in place as he licked her pussy. He was clearly enjoying what he was doing. But when did he do it? And who in the hell was he doing it to? Keyon picked up the remote and skimmed through the rest of the movie; her riding him like a stallion, him sucking her titties. It was a sight to see. Whoever the cameraman was, he was getting everything. The man had gotten so close to Keyon and the unknown female, that you could not only see his dick going in and out with cream on it, you could hear the slurping sounds her soaking wet pussy made.. He couldn't watch anymore.

A note had fallen out of the envelope and lay on his desk. Once he read it, all color drained from his face. *I thought you might want to see what really happened the night of your anniversary party. You really enjoyed yourself, huh? Don't worry. I made sure Symone got a copy of this as well since she was unable to make it. Don't forget to send me a wedding invite. That is, if the wedding is still on after your fiancé sees this.*

He ejected the movie, threw it in his briefcase, grabbed his keys and made a mad dash to the elevator. It was time to go home. The elevator took forever to reach his floor and even longer to get him to the parking garage.

It was a miracle that he didn't get any speeding tickets on his way home because he broke more than one traffic law. As fast as he thought he was moving, things still seemed to be moving in slow motion. Red lights stayed red longer and he seemed to catch everyone going up Peachtree Street. There was an accident on Pharr Road once he made it to Buckhead, which caused even further delay. Darkness had settled over the city that masked all the bright lights. It was the same darkness indicative of the mood that enveloped him. Tears formed in the corners of his eyes. They threatened to spill over. He held them at bay. *I need to focus. I can't let my emotions get in the way of what I need to do. Symone knows me. I would never cheat on her. All I need to do is explain. Once she hears my side of the story, we'll be fine. We can work this out. Can't we?*

When he turned his Jaguar onto Roxboro Road, he could see that all the lights were out in his house at the end of the cul-de-sac. Dread filled his body the closer he got to his home. He pounded his fist on the steering wheel like it was to blame that he was in this mess. *Fuck! Fuck! Fuck!* Putting his hand on the door handle, he opened it slowly, like he didn't want her to hear him. He shut the car door quietly. Nervous hands fumbled for the house key and inserted it into the lock. It was pitch black in the house. Keyon closed the door behind him, shutting out the moonlight that crept in while it was opened. He walked towards the staircase and stumbled over something in the middle of the floor. He used the light on his cell phone to see what he fell over. Luggage. Lots of it. He got up and switched on the lights. He ran upstairs to the master bedroom. No Symone. She wasn't in the kitchen, dining or living rooms. Just when he was about to give up, he heard noise coming from his studio. It was dark there, too. He fumbled for the light switch but couldn't feel it.

"Don't turn on the light. My note said that this DVD is best watched in the dark, preferably with surround sound, with someone you love. I figured hell; I have two out of three so why not go for it? Imagine my surprise when I put it in and saw this. Nice wedding gift for me, huh?"

"Symone. Please let me explain."

"Explain what Keyon? Something told me that you were cheating on me, but *noooo* my ass wanted to believe what everyone told me. That you loved me too much to do me like that. Yeah, right. Like Tina sang, what's love got to do with it?"

"Baby, listen. I don't know what's going on, but this is not the way it looks. I don't know how this happened and I certainly don't know who *she* is," he ended, pointing to the woman on screen.

"Are you going to try to pull some R. Kelly shit here? Tell me that the dude in the video ain't you? Lie and say that it was all photoshopped? Because if you are, you can save it." She went to the big screen TV and pointed at details in the video. "That is your tattoo isn't it? *Hard as Steele.* That ain't common like a rose. And how many dudes you know have *your* granny's name on his arm? Lillian Alma Steele. I'll tell you. NONE! So, you can miss me with all that bullshit, Keyon."

"I'm not saying that that's not me. It is. But I don't know *how* I came to be there. I think someone may have slipped something in my drink at the party."

"Oh, so now you're claiming that defense? Nice try, but

that ain't gon' work either. Look, let's end each other's misery right here and now. Clearly we need some time apart."

"So what, Symone? You packed my bags and making me leave? That's not the way to solve problems."

"Here's yet another example of how much you *don't* pay attention to me. Those are my bags, Keyon. Not yours. Why would I try to make you leave? This is your house."

"Our house. Symone, I was set up. I know that makes me sound like a conspiracy theorist but I'm telling the truth. Yes, that is me in the video, but I have never lied to you or cheated on you. You have to know that. Babe there are people after me. They want to see me dead. *Us* dead," he said, pointing to her and then himself. "Please don't go. Let's work this out."

"I don't have the energy or the desire to work anything out. It's over between us Keyon. Good-bye."

He didn't get up and try to stop her from leaving. There was no changing her mind. It was now clear to him that no matter what he said or did they were over. He had to pay Big. That was the only way to keep her safe. And after his debt was paid, he was going to have to let her go. For good.

• • • • • • • • • • • • • • • • • •

Two hours later, Donnie stroked Symone's hair and rocked her slowly. She allowed her friend to cry in her lap while whispering to her that everything would be all right. Symone left Keyon and didn't have any place to go, so she ran to Donnie, who stood waiting, with open arms. All of her careful planning worked out exactly the way she wanted it to. Keyon and Symone were ruined and Symone was hers. She was going to give her a little time to heal before making her move. Symone wouldn't cry forever. When she stopped, she was going to want someone to love her. Donnie planned on being that one.

• • • • • • • • • • • • • • • • • •

Domynique sat on her cot in the homeless shelter and

read a book. She couldn't believe how Stone had played her. Then again, she could. After the deed was done and she fucked that man, Donnie was supposed to give her the $5000 she promised. But that didn't happen. Instead, Donnie laughed in her face and told her that she never planned on giving her one red cent and that Domynique owed her and she ought to be glad that she was still a free woman. Not that five grand was a helluva lot of money, but Domynique had made a few plans on how she would spend it. She could have paid the rent up on a small, cheap apartment if nothing else. Even if it was in Bankhead. Hell, she just wanted a roof over her head that was hers. Unfortunately, that was just another pipe dream.

• • • • • • • • • • • • • • • • •

Charmaine looked at the scene below with great interest. Symone didn't take heed to all the warnings that she had issued in the past. It was time for Charmaine to make things crystal clear. Donnie would not be acting this way if it wasn't for the other woman, Charmaine reasoned. It was time for Charmaine to teach Symone a lesson in math. First division. Then subtraction.

# The Heat Is On

Some people, unfortunately, have to learn the hard way. Kelly Vanderbilt was one of them. She messed with Donnie a few times during the summer of 2009. Charmaine busted the windows out of her car and took a sledgehammer to the body of her 2008 Mercedes C250. Even still, Kelly didn't catch the hint. The only thing that made her leave Donnie alone was a job offer. She was a bank executive and left Atlanta when World Banc asked her to open a branch in Switzerland. Only a fool would have turned that job down, and Kelly wasn't a fool. But she did do some terribly foolish things. Fucking Donnie, being number one.

She was back in Atlanta for a short vacation to see her family and friends. She added Donnie to her To-Do List while visiting. For the past two nights, Donnie had taken the beautiful Angelina Jolie look-a-like out on the town, and then brought her back to her pussy lair. Symone went to Dallas, Texas to visit some friends for a few days, leaving Donnie to do what she loved best. Fuck. Charmaine knew that Donnie hadn't gotten any from the sexy radio host. She also knew exactly what she was doing. Donnie was going to ingratiate herself to Symone; be the best friend she could be, listen at all hours of the night, and give her a false sense of security until Donnie went in for the kill and turned her out. Charmaine would be watching and waiting for that moment. Right now though, Kelly Vanderbilt was getting under Charmaine's skin.

And Charmaine was about to get under hers.

Charmaine knew that Kelly was a wild sleeper from watching her. What she had in store for the other woman was one of the best ideas she had had to date. Smiling, she slipped on her blue and white pin striped dress and white nursing shoes. She adjusted the housekeeping uniform and put a container on the cart behind the sheets and towels. Kelly stayed all night with Donnie and was still at the house when Charmaine left. She only had a short window of about forty-five minutes before the real housekeeping staff came on duty. She pushed the cart down the hall of the Omni Hotel and parked it in front of room 803.

Once inside, she quickly stripped the bed and put on a sheet she brought with her. *I don't know why hotels only use flat sheets*, she thought. Then she took the lid off of the container and sprinkled its contents onto the sheet, spreading it with a hair brush. Next, she put the flat sheet on followed by the blanket and bedspread. She adjusted the pillows, dusted the furniture and emptied the trash, to make it look like the housekeeper had done her job. Lastly, she called the front desk pretending to be Kelly to tell them that she wouldn't need full housekeeping services that morning, just extra towels. She hurried and returned the cart to the closet, changed back into her clothes and exited the hotel through the service entrance. It only took twenty-five minutes.

● ● ● ● ● ● ● ● ● ● ● ● ● ● ● ● ●

You can say that you slept with Donnie but the truth is you never really *slept*. Donnie had an insatiable appetite and could lick and stay in pussy all night. Because she wore a strap-on, her dick never got soft and even if the pussy dried up from her being in it so long, she kept a tube of lubricant by the bed. Kelly loved that about Donnie because her sex drive rivaled her sexy stud's. But as much as she loved being with her lover, she needed some sleep and the only place she could do that was back at her hotel room. Around 10:00 a.m., she was finally able to detach the other woman's lips from her pearl tongue and head to the hotel.

A nice gush of cold air greeted her when she walked into the room. Housekeeping had cleaned nicely and even left her extra towels. She showered and washed her hair and readied herself for a late morning nap. It didn't take long for her to fall into a deep sleep. She rolled over in her sleep and felt a prick in her thigh. She rubbed the spot and was pricked on her finger by something. Wide-awake now, she tried to roll out of bed but tiny needle-like objects pierced her skin. She was crying by the time she got out of bed. The crying turned to screaming when her skin began to heat up. A porter, who was delivering dry cleaning next door, heard the screams and rushed to see what was going on. He used his passkey to enter the room.

"Housekeeping!" he yelled out, coming through the door.

"In here."

"Yikes!" The porter exclaimed after seeing her reddening skin.

It was also beginning to swell. He called the front desk receptionist who then called 9-1-1. By the time the EMT's arrived, Kelly was complaining of ringing in her ears. Her breathing was rapid and shallow and she was dizzy. Because of the things embedded in her skin, they had to transport her sitting upright on the stretcher until they reached the ambulance. They started an I.V.

The man riding in the back got a specimen cup and a pair of tweezers to pull out one of the foreign objects so the doctors would have something to send to the lab immediately. Fortunately for Kelly, they transported her to Crawford Hospital and the emergency room wasn't swamped. A nurse met the EMT's and got a quick rundown of her vitals and symptoms. He showed the nurse what he had found.

"At first, I didn't know what it was in her skin so I got the tweezers and pulled one out. Look at this," he asked, holding the cup up for her to see.

"Is that a burr?" the nurse asked.

"That's the name of it," he said, snapping his fingers. "I

knew I'd seen it before. This is one of the irritating things that stick in your socks or pant leg when you walk through grass."

"Exactly. So what? The young lady has a few stuck in her leg, is that it?"

"No. She has hundreds stuck in her body. They're in her calves, thighs, buttocks, back and a few in her breasts. It also looks like she has some minor burns."

"Burns? From burrs?"

"That's what we said. But these are not the little fuzzy ones. These are the kinds that look like thorns. But still, something else is going on there. Maybe an allergy."

"Wow. Alright then, thanks fellas. We'll take it from here."

While the lab analyzed the burrs, the staff tended to Kelly. When a registration nurse came in to get some information from the woman, she started to convulse and puke. The vomit had blood in it.

"She's overdosing! Go get sodium bicarb. Stat! What the hell is going on here? And where the hell are those lab reports? Is anyone working today?" A lab technician came while the nurse was barking orders and handed her a report.

"Sharon, I have those labs for you. Weird as shit though. Check'em out."

She read through the report and handed it off to the emergency room physician.

"What the hell? Am I reading this correctly? Methyl Salicylate? Is she an athlete?"

"From what we gathered, she was asleep in a hotel bed and when she rolled over a few hundred burrs pricked her. She suffered third degree burns as well on her thighs and midscection. We've applied burn salve to parts of her skin and administered a Sodium Bicarbonate by IV. She's stable right now."

"This report suggests that the burrs where soaked in oil of wintergreen. If she was asleep when this took place that suggests to me that this was intentional. What did the hotel say?"

"They called the police. According to them, none of their

hotel staff serviced that room, with the exception of leaving towels in the bathroom. It was in and out. The cop that took the report at the hotel is here now if you wish to speak with him, Dr. Murdock."

"I do. I'll go see him now."

"Dr. Murdock, Nurse Dandridge. The patient has bloody stools. The kidney's are in trouble."

The doctor and his staff rushed to Kelly's side to see what was going on. All color had drained from her pretty face and she was still convulsing. There was in fact blood in her stools. She defecated in the bed. They all worked to get Kelly stable, putting her on dialysis. By the time the blood work came back, she still hadn't responded to the treatment. Her breathing had steadied and but she was in an induced coma. The officer was standing in the waiting room when the doctor came out.

"Let's talk in my office, shall we?"

"Sure thing, Doc."

"Doctor Murdock. Coffee?"

"Uh, yeah. Thanks. How's the patient? I'd like to get a statement from her if I can."

"It's still touch and go."

"As soon as I took the report at the hotel, I came right over. I'm Blaire by the way. Sergeant Keenan Blaire." The two men shook hands.

"I have seen this happen before but never like this."

"What is *this*?"

"Sports cream overdose. Sometimes athletes use it in order to relieve pain in their bodies and they rub too much on. They mistakenly believe that the more they use the quicker they will feel better."

"Sports cream?"

"You know? Icy Hot or Ben Gay. The active ingredient is methyl salicylate. This is the most toxic of all salicylates."

"What's the word on Ms. Vanderbilt?"

"It's too soon to tell. Her kidneys are extremely dam-aged. We've done all we can right now. If her kidney's don't respond soon…well, it won't be good. Then there are the burns. We'll have to irrigate them and keep a watchful eye over them to prevent infection. We'll do this for two or three days to see how well she is healing. Hopefully, once the nurses treat her, we won't need to proceed with debridement."

"Debridement?"

"Surgery to remove the burned skin. She is young. I would hate to see her have to go through that. Surgery could leave some pretty ugly scars. She may not feel comfortable wearing a bikini again. But right now, that's the least of our concerns."

"Geesh. This is unreal."

"My sentiments exactly."

"I really need to hear her side of things. We stripped the hotel sheets off the bed for evidence. The sheets my team pulled off didn't belong to the hotel. They were cotton sheets. I figure, whoever did this, used those sheets in order for the burrs to stay in place."

"The burrs were soaked in wintergreen oil and I believe the sheets were wiped with Ben-Gay for extra potency. The lab is running tests now. Some of the burrs we examined here had Ben-Gay cream still in them. When the burrs punctured her skin, the toxin was able to get into the blood stream quicker. My staff removed over 500 of them from her body."

"Hmmm. My team said there were at least a thousand of those things left on the sheets. That's a lot to be stuck in your body. I can't imagine how much pain that would cause."

"Because of her small size and weight, a high amount of toxin absorbed into her system. We will monitor her for the next few days to make sure that she is out of the water. Whoever did this wanted to make sure she suffered. It was almost as if they were…"

"They were what, Doctor?"

"Sending a message."

The men left the confines of the office and went to check on Kelly. A nurse was administering pain medication through her IV when they walked in. Detective Blair stared down at the sleeping beauty and wondered what type of psycho would do something like this. He was almost lost in thought when the nurse said, "she's coding, Doctor."

"I'm going to need you to leave, Detective." That was an order.

He stepped into the hallway and headed towards the waiting room. An interracial couple rushed to the nurse's station and asked about Kelly. A nurse pointed them in his direction.

"Ma'am, Sir, I'm Detective Blair. I was first on the scene when the call came in. I'm sorry this is happening, but I assure you, we will catch whoever did this."

"What is going on with my baby?" her mother cried.

"Yes, will someone please explain what's happening with our daughter?"

"I don't know much," Keenan began, "but the doctor said it's an overdose of some kind."

"Overdose! Why that's preposterous. My little girl hasn't done drugs a day in her life."

"No, she didn't do drugs but the doc…" Just then, the emergency room doors swung open and the doctor came over to her parents.

"Mr. and Mrs. Vanderbilt. My staff and I are doing all that we can to stabilize your daughter. My nurse will explain what's going on. I have to go back in now."

"Yo, Doc. Lemme know when it's cool to question her. I gotta get it while it's hot."

"An appropriate choice of words to use regarding a burn victim, Detective. How very tactless of you," the doctor said with disgust.

Keenan sat down in the chair and waited for his chance to go question his only witness. He had a job to do just like the doctor did. The latest Essence Magazine sat on the table in front of him so he picked it up and started flipping through the pages. Only when he heard a loud wail did he realize he'd fallen asleep. The doctor was at the other end of the hall talking to

Kelly's parents and a nurse came to talk to him. Kelly went into renal failure and he wouldn't be able to interview her after all. She was dead.

# Deadly Intent.

Morgan Calloway was a pest. Charmaine hated pests. Therefore, Charmaine hated Morgan Calloway. She was one of the women who Donnie couldn't seem to get enough of. And lately it seemed that every time she turned on her surveillance equipment Donnie was talking to her. She always had a goofy smile when she was on the phone with her. Unfortunately, Morgan always booked hotel rooms to rendezvous with Donnie. Leaving Charmaine in the dark regarding the number of times the two had been together. But it was well over twenty times, making them more than friends. It infuriated her knowing that Donnie was fucking around on her with a woman she knew nothing about or had ever seen. Not until yesterday.

The other day, for the very first time, Donnie said Morgan's last name over the phone. Calloway. Immediately, Charmaine Googled the name to find that Morgan was the pretty ex-wife of a hot Academy Award winning actor, Randall Calloway. Their pictures were plastered all over the Internet. Once she had her name and a photo she was able to begin her research. She always learned as much as she could about a subject before pursuing anything.

As she looked down at the writing tablet and reviewed her findings, she couldn't help but get butterflies in her stomach. She was excited and angry at the same time. Somehow, someway, Morgan had become a significant part of Donnie's life and Charmaine just couldn't have that. Right now, Morgan was just a temporary problem, who was about to be handled with a permanent solution. *Fuck her once, shame on me. Fuck her twice, shame on you.*

● ● ● ● ● ● ● ● ● ● ● ● ● ● ● ● ●

Morgan stood in front of the mirror in the women's fitting room at Saks Fifth Avenue in Phipps Plaza and her mind traveled back in time. It was there, three months ago, where she first met Donnie who was working in loss prevention. From the moment she walked into the store, Donnie's eyes never left her. The two had an instant connection. For a whole week, Morgan came to the store just to lay eyes on the sexy stud.

The day she finally spoke to Stone, she was giddy and nervous like a schoolgirl. After their brief conversation, Morgan went to the dressing room to try on a dress. A few minutes later Donnie knocked on her dressing room door and Morgan answered. Naked. Stunned at first, Donnie stood there, licking her lips like LL Cool J, before she asked Morgan if she was okay. Giggling, Morgan nodded and pulled Donnie inside the private space.

Without speaking, Morgan kissed her, allowing herself to be overcome with passion as Donnie kissed her back. It didn't take long to get her out of her clothes. Donnie sat Morgan in the chair and kissed her ankles, her calves then worked her way up to her inner thighs before nestling her face between the woman's legs. She stroked, sucked and nibbled on the pearl tongue until Morgan shook with pleasure. It took every muscle in Morgan's body not to scream out because if she did, both she and Donnie would go to jail for lewd acts in a public place. The tongue felt so good inside of Morgan. Donnie didn't rush. She took her time, licking slowly, familiarizing her tongue with the taste of the woman who sat before her. Donnie's tongue made circles around Morgan's clit and she sucked the hard button, applying just enough pressure to stimulate her new lady friend. Morgan's hips writhed in the seat like a washing machine agitator. She was pleased and pissed at the same time because Donnie would bring her to the brink and then back off. Morgan wasn't used to this kind of teasing but she was used to getting her pussy licked like a champ. Her ex-husband used to take good care of her in that department. But he no longer mattered. He was her past. Donnie Stone was her future.

Randy just didn't 'get her' and that was the real reason their relationship had failed. But Donnie understood her and she was happy that the two of them had met. Morgan thought that Donnie had changed her for the better. She was very much in love and tonight she was determined to show her just how much.

An hour and a half later she had exited Phipps Plaza with two garment bags and headed to her car in the underground parking deck. She wanted to get something special for Donnie but wasn't sure what. The stud wasn't very picky and Morgan knew that she could buy something from the West End Mall and Donnie would be appreciative. As Morgan approached her car she noticed an extremely handsome guy walking her way.

He was average height for a man but he was dressed to the nines and wearing handmade Berluti shoes which made Morgan give him a double take. Normally, he would be the type of man that Morgan would be interested in. But even as fine and well groomed as he was, all she could think about was Donnie. She wasn't surprised when he approached her.

"Excuse me, but can you help me? I think I am lost?" he asked.

"Sure. Where are you trying to go?" She asked after putting her things in the trunk and closing it.

"Well, the sales clerk at Bottega Veneta was trying to give me directions to the West End, but I don't think she really knew what she was talking about. I ended up in the exact same place I started from."

"How funny, I was just thinking about going to the West End myself. You can follow me. Where exactly in the West End are you going?"

"Oh, I'm headed to a thrift store down there. I have a

bunch of things that I want to donate. I just moved here and realized that I still have things with the tags on it that I will never wear. Might as well give them to someone who will make good use of them."

"I was looking for some nice inexpensive things to give to my friend. Mind if I take a look?"

"Sure," the handsome stranger said. "My SUV is right over here. By the way, my name is Franklin. What's yours?"

"Morgan. Morgan Stone." She answered, giving him Donnie's surname. "So, what all do you have in here?" She asked as they approached the back of a Porsche Cayenne Turbo. "This is nice. Yours?"

"The wife's," Franklin replied. "I drive a souped up station wagon on 26-inch rims. I'm just playing. I just got it a few days ago. Still trying to learn how this thing ticks."

"Well, it's very nice at any rate. So let me see what you have."

Franklin lifted up the gate and revealed several boxes and bags of new and used garments that were marked for the Salvation Army. Morgan began going through each piece, admiring the man's taste in clothing. He had over ten thousand dollars in brand new and used stuff that could have gotten top dollar if he tried to sell it. But since Morgan didn't have a benevolent bone in her body, she found it hard to comprehend that anyone would just 'give' valuable stuff like that away. At the bottom of the last bag she found several bottles of cologne that had very expensive labels on them.

"You're giving these away, too?"

"Yep. My ex gave them to me and I don't want any reminders of her around anymore. Take a sniff and see if you like it. If so, take it to your friend. He'll thank you later."

Morgan obliged and opened a pretty bottle and took a whiff of it. The scent was faint so she put the bottle closer to her nose and inhaled deeply. She immediately got light headed and dropped the bottle. Franklin stepped behind Morgan and tazed her, causing her to stumble and then pulled a handkerchief out of his pocket and covered her face, knocking her out. Franklin moved the bags out of the way and threw Morgan's unconscious body inside. He covered her with bags and boxes and closed the gate to the truck.

A few minutes later, a pretty woman, who could have easily been mistaken for Morgan came up to Franklin and he gave her Morgan's car keys and she gave him an envelope containing twenty grand. The woman got in the car and drove off. In less than three hours, the Aston Martin DB7 was tucked safely away in a garage in Birmingham, Alabama, and by morning, it would have a new VIN, a new color, a new title and a new owner.

Meanwhile, Franklin drove Morgan to an abandoned warehouse near Fulton Industrial Boulevard, an area in Atlanta known for prostitution and nefarious deeds. He pulled up to a garage door, got out, lifted it and then got in the car and drove through. Once he had parked inside he let the garage door down and locked it. Franklin lifted the truck's gate and transferred Morgan to a wheelchair, strapped her in, and rolled her to a small office. By the time she woke up she had been out for almost two hours.

"Well, well, well, if it ain't Sleeping Beauty. You've been out for quite a while. How did you sleep?" he asked maniacally.

"Where am I? What have you done to me?" Morgan said fearfully. She looked around the tiny room and saw a brown desk with a black medical bag sitting on it.

"Don't start with the twenty questions. By the way, remind me next time not to use pure Ether. I really didn't want you knocked out so long. But any who, how are you?"

"Who are you and why are you doing this?"

"I'll answer your questions all in due time. I just need to put a few things in place."

When he left the room, Morgan was tried desperately to pick the lock on the handcuffs. Franklin shook his head at the pathetic sight before him as he peeked through the door. While she was knocked out, he went through her purse and found a poem of sorts that Donnie had written to the other woman. At first, Franklin was going to just do some irreparable damage to Morgan's face but reading that note made his blood boil until he snapped. Morgan had to go. The boots he wore didn't make a sound as he crossed the concrete floor towards Morgan.

"*Morgan you know I'm feelin u,*" he began reading. "*I wanna feel u while the rain beatz up against the roof drummin to our rhythm as our bodies grasp each other in the thunderous night. Feels alright to me. Touch me. Taste me. Feel me. Be with me. Be in me. Be on me. Take me in u. Let me have u, forever, never-ending, Baby oil soft skin u possess to provoke my sense of smells. Mind blowing. Do u mind if I lie between your thighs and press passionately up against your inner most seducing juices? Ooh this has got to be heaven cuz u got me open like 7-11. Keep it goin' like on and on, do u hear that? Those are the sounds of love makin' cummin' from your room. What are we waiting for? Go higher than we've ever been before. Ur mine and I'm ur's.*"

"Now ain't that some shit? Yo' ass must be pretty got damned special to have someone writing all this mushy shit to you. You think you all that, bitch?"

"If your ass wasn't so deranged then maybe someone would write you a love note, too."

"Oh. So you wanna talk shit? Yep. I'm deranged. Glad you noticed. I've known I was crazy for years. But I have some-one who loves me. As a matter of fact, the same person who claims to love you is the same person who claims to love me as well."

"What the fuck are you talking about? I'm in love with a woman who *only* loves women. She wouldn't give your ass the time of day."

"You are so fucking clueless. You must have been a blonde in your former life, dumb ass. I must admit, I am quite jealous because Donnie has never said to me what she told you in the next note. Let's read it, shall we?"

"*Have a safe trip home...I know you're gone by now, but*

*I will give u a to be continued email so when u hit me in the morning you have somethin' to feed off of. Ur welcome anytime, anywhere, make yourself at home in my love. Get naked and lay in ecstasy...touch me in that place you know will drive me to enter your gates with Thanksgiving(lol). Oooh make me feel like I'm the only person u've ever wanted and needed, like I am your every desire, let me put you in a position that you will never forget who we are together, cuz there's no I in We and We are definitely 2 and 1 in the same, be my lifetime valentine. I love wut we're doin and I know that one day we will have to limit what "WE" currently means, but for now, I'ma enjoy to the last drop like Maxwell. Can u imagine wut it would be like if there was a male version of me? You would be married and taken away from hell, this hell we call Atlanta, away from all the haters...come with me, lets run away and find ourselves wrapped up in sensuality. Ur sexiness has caught my eye in such a way that I can't tear away from u and I don't want to... I'd love to stay here forever...I love you!"*

There was a short pause before he found his voice, which was changing with every word he spoke. "She would get you pregnant if she could, but since she can't, I am sure that she would try to talk you into getting pregnant the old fashioned way, and the two of you raising that baby together. She has always wanted a baby. That's why you have to go because as much as I have to offer her, I can never give her that. I would never be able to compete with you, let alone win. And I hate losing. I won't lose," he finished morosely.

"What the hell is this? Why do you sound like a woman?" Morgan pleaded with her captor softly. "Please listen to me. My husband will give you whatever you want. I'm Morgan Calloway. He's worth millions. Just please let me go. I promise I won't go to the cops."

"Yo' ex ain't paying shit and Donnie is too busy licking the next bitch's pussy to worry about you."

"Stone loves me. She would never cheat on me. I don't know who you are or what this is but-"

"But nothing, bitch. Her blood type is ho- negative. It's impossible for her to be faithful to anyone. Not me…you. Not even that home-wreckin' ass Symone. Now hold still. I have something for you. This won't hurt but it may sting slightly," he said as he injected her with the contents of the vials. Morgan's eyes darted left to right as the poisons began to course through her veins.

"Let me go. I swear when I get out of here I am going to fuck you up!"

"Such bravado. It won't do you any good. Soon enough the world will be minus one less skank. Morgan tried to lift her arm but it felt like lead. She couldn't talk either. Slowly, tears ran down her face.

"Don't fight it. You can't win. It's Saxitoxin. In a few minutes, your whole body will be numb."

Morgan sat paralyzed. All she could do was watch the crazy person move about the room with purpose. Franklin had placed a sixty gallon steel drum on a drum induction heater that looked like a giant electric burner. He poured sodium hydroxide in the barrel and waited for it to heat. The temperature of the lye solution was three-hundred two degrees exactly. The young person smiled, thinking about the end result of the project. In a few hours the contents that would go into the barrel would be no more. All traces of evidence eradicated. No one would know what the drum once contained.

Although Morgan was motionless, all of her sensory motions were still intact. She could still feel pain. Shortly, she would feel lots of it. The barrel was only a quarter full but it was enough to start the process. Franklin lifted Morgan out of the wheelchair over his shoulder and put her feet into the barrel first. The acid began to burn her feet and lower calves. Morgan made inaudible noises. With her flesh virtually melting away, she collapsed inside in an uncomfortable heap but Franklin kept her arms outside of the barrel.

Two bottles of hydrochloric acid were poured into the barrel and then sodium hydroxide powder was poured into the liquid. The room filled with a pig-like, high pitched squeal as the chemicals began to burn the flesh off of Morgan. When it was clear that she was dead, Franklin took an electric knife, held one of Morgan's hands over the barrel and cut her hand off. He was careful not to get any blood on the floor. He dropped the hand into a five gallon paint bucket that had lemon, lime, orange and grapefruit peels in it and then proceeded to cut off the other one in the same fashion.

"Two down, one to go." He held the woman's long hair straight up so that he could get a clear view of her neck and slowly, he began cutting until the only thing that was holding the head on the body was cartilage. The blade on the knife was dulling but Franklin used some elbow grease to detach the final member from his victim. The head was dropped into the bucket. There was a smoke cloud beginning to hover over the drum. Toxic. Deadly. The cloud was so thick, the killer did not see the blood spatter on the outside of the barrel or the ring that rolled under the desk.

Franklin went to the hidden camera and stopped the tape. A huge smile spread across his face. He reached up with his right hand and scratched behind his ear until he felt the prosthetic face begin to peel. He pulled it completely off, put it in the barrel and watched it melt like butter. Another job well done.

No longer in disguise, Charmaine took a brush out of her bag and brushed her hair. Then she grabbed the handle of the paint bucket and took it to the truck. She sat it in the back seat and strapped it in so that it would not tip over. It was dark by the time she parked and walked down the street towards her attic apartment. All the lights were off. No one was home yet. With the exception of a few gangbangers, no one was outside. She went around to the back door, used her key and went inside. Once she was secure, she sat the bucket down, pulled her pants down and used the bathroom in it.

"How does it feel to be shitted on, Morgan? Not good, huh?" She giggled, picking up a photo of Donnie. "It won't be long baby until it's just the two of us again. I love you."

She made sure her equipment was functioning properly and that it was recording, then laid down on her pallet and sang herself to sleep.

*"Oh where, oh where has my little Mo' gone? Oh where, oh where can she be? With her head cut off and her hands all gone, oh where, oh where can she be?"*

# Looking For Love In All The Wrong Places

The nation's prisons were full of innocent people, falsely convicted on the words of people who had their own agenda's or self-serving purpose. Convicted by words. No other evidence. Just words. Keyon was falsely convicted, too, by a sex tape. He was trapped in a cage of guilt and confusion, a self-imposed prison, and only one person held the key. The beautiful mysterious woman he made love to in the video. He watched the tape dozens of times now and saw how he savored the taste of her and how he gently caressed her skin. Even when he entered her, he moved slower than he did than when he was with Symone. That was one of the first things he noticed when he saw the DVD. He knew that Symone had noticed that, too.

With them, their lovemaking had become hurried. The last year or so of their relationship had become boring, almost stagnant. The romance, communication and fun were all gone. Like robots, they moved through the house, barely speaking, and rarely touching.

But the mystery woman was different. Keyon felt this odd connection to her. He didn't know her and had never seen her before, but he wanted to see her again. She was a vision of loveliness. The video didn't show much of her face but he could tell she was a looker. She never stood up but she was much smaller than his six-nine, 215-pound frame. She was thick and curved in all the right places. But Keyon knew that no matter what type of drugs he was on, his psyche knew that chick had some very good pussy because when he turned over with her, changing positions, he did not pull out and that had *never* happened before.

And there lied the guilt and confusion.

He felt guilty because he didn't desire Symone anymore. Instead, he longed for the woman on the video; a woman who was so instrumental in ruining his engagement. A woman who could possibly be on Big's payroll. Oddly enough, he felt that she had saved him. And for that he had to find her. He had to know why she would help someone carry out such a plan against him. What had he done to deserve this? More importantly, he needed her to let him make love to her again, because she casted a spell over him, and his dick got hard just thinking about her. Every time he watched what he now called 'their tape' he beat his meat. He would come so hard, with such violence that he would spill a shit load of his seed but he still couldn't reach satisfaction.

Judy gave him a number to a private detective who was a friend of hers who was known for his discretion and success rate. Keyon needed help finding this woman and fast. Because if he didn't find her soon, he wouldn't have any skin left on his dick. He grabbed the paper and dialed the number, drumming his fingers while he waited for the call to connect, breathing a sigh of relief when a live voice came through the receiver.

•••••••••••••••••••

The lovers laid down slowly on the 1500 thread count, Egyptian cotton sheets. Two beautiful brown bodies in contrast with the stark white sheets. Tongues wrestled with one another, as if doing battle. Soft hands slowly moved over the hard muscled chest. Butterfly kisses traced the man's torso, going downward. The man lying on his back spread his legs, to allow his lover a comfortable spot between them, to pleasure him better. Cold, wet lips wrapped hungrily around his hard dick. Saliva ran down the tool while the tongue licked the nine-inch lollipop. The hungry tongue circled the head of the shaft before it was sucked down the throat.

"That's right, baby. You know how I like it don't you? Grip my dick hard and suck it at the same time. Spit on it and get it nice and wet. Yes, that's it. Stroke it. Ah, yes." The happy man said as he grinded his hips into his lover's mouth. Greedily, his dick was consumed until the creamy load that built up like a geyser inside him, shot out and slid down his lover's throat.

"Are you ready for the chocolate?" he asked his submissive lover but did not wait for a response. Instead, he flipped the heart shaped ass over and rubbed his dick up and down. His condom-wrapped dick was well lubed with Astroglide and his vibrating cock ring was in place. He looked down at the feast he was about to devour and spread the butt cheeks wide so he could have a clear, unobstructed view while he hit it.

"Ah, shit. You're so tight," he managed to groan out. He took long, steady strokes, savoring this. It had been a while since the two of them had been together and he wanted to enjoy it. The cock ring began to feel better with each stroke and Charles picked up the pace.

"Siren, I wanna do some push-ups. Get into position," Charles demanded.

Siren obliged. A pillow was placed on the floor as Charles's lover lay with her back touching the floor and legs in the air, over the shoulders. Charles, who kept his feet on the edge of the bed, got into the push-up position and inserted his dick in the hole. Down, up, down, up. The man exercised his arms and his cock at the same time.

"Mmm, hmm. Yes. That's it, baby. Ooh, your dick feels so good, Chucky. Work it out, baby." Sweat dripped onto Sirens face as Charles went to work in the slick hole. His nuts swung, hitting the ass he was pounding into.

"Shit. I'm getting ready to cum. You ready for this?" He yelled as he shot a hot load into the condom that was still impaled in his lover. He pulled out, but his dick was still rock hard. Charles lifted Siren up to reveal the hardness of his dick.

"You see this shit?" he said, pointing at the bluish-purple

veins that protruded in this dick. "And this?" he asked, showing the engorged head of his shaft that looked like a mushroom cap. Siren nodded yes to both questions.

"Well, this is what you do to me. I can never seem to get enough of you. Now get up here and let your man make love to you."

Siren laid back into the comfort of the down pillows. Charles slowly kissed and caressed Siren and stroked the soft thighs below him. He spread the legs like they were wings and slid inside the wetness that was still present. With each stroke, Charles arched his back and entered. He looked like he was doing the butterfly stroke on dry land. His ass cheeks tightened with each thrust upward and he put his arms under Sirens shoulders so he could pull Siren closer as he penetrated the intimate cavern. Heavy panting and slurping noises from wet kisses filled the room. Charles grinded in circles, trying to go as deep as he could. Rising up on his knees, he grabbed his lover by the shoulders and pulled down until his dick couldn't go in any further and then he began to fuck the shit out of Siren.

"Play with your shit while I fuck you. That shit drives me wild," Charles said between gritted teeth. "Damn. I need to punish you for keeping me waiting on you. You know I need you. Take this dick, you teasing wench. Ooh, ah. Shit!" A few long, hard thrusts later and Charles came again for the second time. This time, he kept his dick inside the tight pocket until he was sure he was satiated and his dick went limp.

"I love it when you call me, Siren. But why do you? I know you know my name."

"I call you Siren because when you cum you make a sound like one."

"Fuck you, Charles."

"You just did."

"Whatever, silly. But seriously, Charles, I've been doing some thinking."

"Ah, shit. We both know how dangerous that can be," he said jokingly. "What you been thinking about, though?"

"Us. I want to tell my friends and family about us."

Charles rolled quickly on his side and said "What? You can't do that. You could ruin me."

"Ruin you? How? Because I tell my people that I have finally found a man that I love who makes me happy in and out of bed and makes me scream like a siren?"

"Exactly. No. I mean. Listen, to me. You have me stumbling over my words here," he said and exhaled. "You know how I feel about you. I care deeply about you and what we have together. But you can't tell anyone about us because there isn't supposed to *be* an us."

"Oh, I get it. You're ashamed of me, aren't you?"

"Where the hell you get that idea from? You know I love you! Come on now, babe. Let's not do this after what we just shared. We're supposed to be resting up, rubbing on each other, getting ready for round two."

"Well, if that's not it then what is it? Why is that I am good enough to sex, but not good enough to see? In public, you don't even acknowledge me and that hurts."

"Look, I know when I was out the other day and I saw you with your friends, I should have said something. But I was with my family and I didn't want to get busted for looking at you with desire in my eyes. I am not ashamed of you. I really do love you. Just give me a lil' time to settle things at home first. I promise you won't be sorry. Now come here and spoon with me. My dick is getting hard," Charles stated as he pulled his lover into him.

They lay there quietly, grinding in a spoon position until he was fully erect again. He parted his lover's cheeks and slid in easily. There was a sense of urgency between the two lovers that wasn't there before. It was always like that after they had *that* talk. Charles wasn't ready to tell his family. Wasn't quite ready to leave the comfort of his other life just yet. Siren knew about the man's other life. Other family. But couldn't help falling in love with him anyway. Charles pumped like a mad man and nutted all over his lover's back side.

*Just give me a little more time baby. I promise, I won't hurt you.* Charles had mumbled before he drifted into a deep, coma-like sleep.

*You already have,* Devine thought. *You already have.*

# Let's Get It On

Lights. Camera. Action. The stage was set. The candles casted a soft a glow around the room. Soft pink rose petals were scattered around the room. The scent of Hawaiian Ginger permeated the air. Everything was in place.

Condoms. Check.

Moet. Check.

Strawberries. Double Check.

All that was missing was her. And she was on her way. On the other side of the bathroom door was the fantasy Donnie had been waiting for. Symone.

It had been almost a month since she'd left Keyon and even though that was the longest Donnie had ever waited to fuck anyone, she knew that Symone would be worth the wait. She knew that it was only a matter of time before the other woman began to see the great qualities she possessed. All the late night talks, acts of chivalry and the 'platonic' dates had paid off. A couple of days ago, Symone kissed Donnie so passionately after they shared a dessert under the stars at Centennial Park in downtown Atlanta. Who knew that a simple sundae under the stars would yield those kinds of results?

Wind Down Wednesday was a great way to make it over the hump of a strenuous workweek. Showcasing local and national bands, people could come out, find a nice spot on the plush green grass, and enjoy the sights and sounds of Atlanta. Donnie packed a blanket and threw a few treats into a picnic basket and prepared to escort Symone there, who surprisingly, had never been.

"I can't believe that a radio host as popular as yourself has never experienced Wind Down Wednesday. What have you been doing?" Donnie questioned as they packed and readied to go downtown.

"I've been so busy working on my career that I haven't had much time for simple pleasures."

"Okay. I can understand that. But damn, your ex is in the music industry. Off the top of my head, I know a few of his acts who have played at the park. He never asked you to come out and chill with him?"

"Well," Symone began hesitantly. "He wanted us to do to that and many more things but like I said, I was too busy working on my career."

"I feel ya', Ma. So, why did you decide to finally come?"

"Because you asked," she replied shyly.

"Damn, that's all it took? Well hell, I should have asked you long time ago. Now, let's go before we end up sitting way over by the playground. I like to sit as close to the music pit as possible. Something about music that turns me on."

"Me too."

"I can imagine. You and old boy must have burned the bed up every night considering his love for music."

"Keyon and I hadn't made love in a while. It's been almost three months since I came."

"Three long months since you came? You mean you ain't been tickling the clit yourself? Shee-it, you prolly got cobwebs in your shit."

"You're stupid. I probably do, though. After being with Keyon, I decided that I wouldn't masturbate anymore. He was the only one I wanted to make me cum; too bad he couldn't say the same. I still can't believe that damned video. It makes me so fucking angry."

"Look, Ma. Don't trip. Forget about him and the porno. Let's just chill and make tonight our night. Is that cool with you?"

"You know it is."

The two women left Symone's apartment and headed towards the park. Symone moved out of Donnie's place a few short days after she left Keyon. She'd taken a mini-vacay to clear her head and rethink some things in her life. When she came back, Donnie took her apartment hunting and showed her a nice complex in the upscale area of Vining's. The apartment was luxurious and expensive. Donnie knew that if she could talk Symone into getting that place, she could talk her into anything. After all, a fool and her money are soon parted. And soon, Symone would be a fool for Donnie. Very soon in fact.

Once they arrived at the park, Donnie found a nice spot under a tree near the sound stage. It was a comfortable warm day in September and the people were out in masses. A jazz band took the stage and began to play the timeless, smooth sounds of Al Jarreau and Najee. Symone rested her head on Donnie's shoulder, closed her eyes, and let the music pour over her like honey. It felt so good to be with someone who didn't judge her and tell her how big of a fool she was for leaving Keyon. Donnie was on Symone's side and that was what she needed. Jynx and Devine made it known that they didn't support her decision to leave Keyon or getting with Donnie.

She knew that Jynx would have a lot to say since she and Keyon were related, but she didn't know that the break-up would cause such a schism between the two friends. Jynx stopped talking to her when she told her about the DVD. But of course, Keyon already told her his side of the story first, and like usual, she sided with him. And so did Devine. Neither of them could understand why she wouldn't give Keyon a chance to prove his innocence to her. Jynx said that her suspicions of him cheating on her in the past made her biased and that she wasn't giving him a fair shot. It was all a bunch of bullshit.

What really shocked Symone was Devine's dislike for Donnie. Once Symone introduced Donnie to her closest friends, she thought they would like her as much as she did, and they would all become fast friends. Mistakenly, she thought that when they saw how happy she was, they would be happy in return. The four of them would be able to hang out and kick it. But Devine had been cold and distant to Donnie when they were introduced and pulled Symone to the side to tell her that crossing the line with a lesbian was not a wise thing to do. Particularly, that one.

"Honey, I don't know how much you know about this chick, but trust me, this ain't what you want."

"How in the hell are you going to tell me about fucking with a girl when you lay up with a different dude every weekend?"

"Now you wait just a damn minute, Symone. I'm trying to look out for you not judge you. I could give a flying fuck who you let lick your pussy. But this chick is bad news and you need to be careful."

"You don't even know her. How you gon' pass judgment like that?"

"I may not know her personally, Sweet-tart; but I do know a thing or two about her. The community is not that big at all. I heard bad things about her from her past lovers."

"Right. Past lovers. They are nothing but bitter bitches who are angry that she dumped their ugly asses. She and I aren't even fucking and bitches are jealous of our friendship."

"*Yet.* You're not fucking, *yet.* But it's coming, trust me. It's at the top of her 'to do' list."

"Whatever, Devine. Just because you can't be friends with a straight man without wanting to fuck him, doesn't mean that I can't be friends with a gay chick without wanting to fuck her. I expected this from Jynx, but I thought you of all people would understand."

That night did not go the way Symone had imagined it at all. That was two weeks ago. Since then, her conversation with her friends had been extremely limited. But Donnie was right there to pick up the slack. She didn't trip off the things Devine had told Symone. She just told Symone that Devine was just looking out for her and trying to protect his friend. Donnie said that she would have done the same thing if the sho were on the other foot. That's why Symone loved Donnie, because she was always looking at the good in people and making all the negatives, positive. *Love?* Did she really think that? Could she be in love with a woman?

For the past couple of months, Symone and Donnie had been nothing more than friends. Symone sat many nights watching Donnie get ready for her dates. She was so considerate and romantic. No matter who the lady was, Donnie always had a rose. Even though they didn't date, Symone knew first-hand what type of person Donnie was. She always held the door open for her, opened the car door and pulled out her chair. Donnie was kind and generous and was genuinely interested in what Symone had going on. And that night at Wind Down Wednesday was no different.

Donnie managed to keep a caramel sundae cold and semi-firm by using dry ice. Symone mentioned in passing how caramel sundaes were her favorite. She was surprised that Donnie even remembered. Symone smiled from ear to ear when Donnie pulled the ice cream out of the insulated picnic basket. With great care, Donnie spooned the sweet cream into Symone's hot and waiting mouth. As she fed her, she looked deep into Symone's eyes, sending subliminal messages to her friend. The pounding of the drums caused Donnie's steady hand to waiver and ice cream fell on Symone's lips and cleavage.

Slowly, Donnie leaned over and licked the ice cream off the top of Symone's left breast. Then she licked slowly up her collarbone, neck, until finally reaching her bottom lip. Symone parted her lips and allowed the velvety smooth tongue to delve into the warmth of her mouth. The kiss was so soft and sensual that it made her clit jump. The kiss deepened when Symone opened her mouth to allow Donnie the chance to explore further. Oblivious to the stares around them or the fact that they were in a very public place, the two kissed for another minute or so before breaking apart.

"We'd like to thank you all for coming out and enjoying the last Wind Down Wednesday with us. Be safe going home and we will see you all right here, next year," the announcer said.

"Next year? What did she mean next year?" Symone questioned.

"Well, Boo. This runs April through September. This is the last Wednesday in September so it's done for the year."

"Man, that sucks. How they gon' play me like that? I just discovered this."

"Yeah, it's pretty cool. But I will bring you every Wednesday next year as soon as its time."

"Next year, huh? We're still gonna be friends that long?"

"More than that if you let me. I know you know how I feel about you."

"Yeah. I do. I feel the same way about you, too, D. I have for a while now."

"Word?"

"Word. As a matter of fact, I am ready to become yours in every sense of the word."

Donnie could have jumped up and clicked her heels but she played it cool. When she took Symone back to her apartment they kissed a little more but Donnie wanted to wait to make it special for her. So now here they were, getting ready to cross the line from friends to lovers.

While Donnie sat in the bed, stroking her strap-on, Symone, fidgeted on the other side of the bathroom door, contemplating the decision she was making. Questioning if she was doing the right thing. Not the fact that she was getting ready to make love to a woman, but that she was about to make love to someone other than Keyon. Five years was a long time to be with one person and she was scared of the newness of it all. But she did love Donnie. More than that, she was *in love* with her and tonight, she was going to show her how much.

When the door opened, Donnie stopped stroking herself and stood up to admire the sexy woman who walked towards her. Symone's shoulder length asymmetrical bob made her look stylish and sexy at the same time and it moved as easily as she did. Standing face to face, the two women saved the words for later. At that moment, none were needed. Donnie took her right hand and traced the outlines of Symone's face, caressing the soft skin of her face and neck. She pulled her closer to her own face until their lips were barely touching. Donnie's tongue flicked Symone's lips and then she bit down gently on the bottom one, sucking it into her mouth.

Symone responded by sliding her own tongue into Donnie's mouth and let her tongue wrestle with her lover's. Donnie broke the kiss and nibbled the spot behind Symone's ear and played with her titties at the same time. She walked her back to the bed and slid the black lace negligee over her head, exposing her bare breasts.

Next, she removed her matching panties and discarded them on the floor before sitting her down on the bed. Donnie propped Symone up on several pillows, got in the bed next to her, and began kissing her again. She rolled Symone's hard nipples around between her thumb and index finger. It was feeling so good that Symone started grinding her hips in the mattress. Soon, long fingers found her moist center and started going in and out in a rhythmic motion. The more she moaned the harder Donnie kissed and finger fucked her. She was getting very wet. Donnie used her thumb to rub the hard nub and three other fingers to penetrate the slick box. Symone's hips bucked as she came in her girlfriend's hand.

Donnie, who had only just begun, slid down on the bed and instructed Symone to sit on her face and hold on to the headboard. Nervously, Symone, did as she was told. This was going to be her first time ever having her pussy eaten by a woman. When Donnie's tongue first touched her, Symone jumped a bit at the shock that she felt. Not to be deterred, Donnie reached up and grabbed Symone's hips so she sat securely in position, and then she began to lick with vigor. Getting into the groove of it, Symone settled into place and began to gyrate on her woman's face, whipping the pussy on her. Donnie sucked and slurped on the pussy until Symone came in her mouth.

"I gottta get a better look at my pussy," Donnie said, turning Symone over. With her index and middle fingers, she spread Symone's lips apart, revealing the pink flesh between them. "Look at that shit. It's like eating a Twinkie. You all creamy in the middle. I want my face all up in that shit," she said taking a nosedive into her creamy dessert.

"Oh, yes. Suck this pussy, Donnie. I love it. Yes," Symone whimpered.

"I got something for yo' ass, 'Mone. Turn over and get on your knees." Donnie, who always wore a strap-on, slid a condom on the fake dick and shoved it into Symone's pussy and started pounding away. She fucked and fingered her at the same time, playing with her clit, getting her worked up. Donnie reached on the bedside table and grabbed a small vibrator. Using the juices from Symone's body, she wet the vibrator and inserted it into Symone's ass.

"Ouch! That hurts, baby. What is that? Please take it out." Symone squealed.

"Just go with it. You'll adjust in a minute, trust me. I'ma 'bout to make you feel like that nigga never could. You gone see today, baby. I waited a long time to please you. Now, take this dick in your ass. That's it. Grind that shit, you nasty bitch."

Symone was horrified by the way Donnie spoke to her and turned on at the same time. The small dildo was vibrating and causing pulsating shocks to travel through her entire body. Her clit was throbbing and juices flowed.

"Ah, yes. Fuck this pussy and my ass baby. You're turning me out, Donnie. Fuck! I need you."

Their bodies slapped one another as Donnie pumped into her pussy and continued to fuck her ass with the dildo.

"Shit, I'm about to cum," Donnie yelled. Symone was too and reached around and grabbed Donnie's ass in an attempt to take in more dick. Beads of sweat dripped onto Symone's back as she buried her head into the pillow to muffle her screams.

"I-am-cum-ming!" Symone cried out. Donnie growled like a wild animal and banged her lover's ass until she found her own release and collapsed on top of her.

"That was amazing, Donnie. No one has ever made me feel like you just did."

"No one?" Donnie asked.

"No one. I came harder and longer than I ever have in my life."

"I'm glad you're satisfied, Ma. I aim to please."

"Well, I'm more than satisfied, baby. I'm a woman in love."

"You're what?"

"Um, I love you, Donnie."

"Sho' nuff?"

"Yes, baby. I do."

"Damn, 'Mone. You don't know how long I been waiting to hear those words. I love you too, girl."

"Really?"

"Yes, really. How could you think otherwise? I been trying to show you all these months."

"Well, you were also taking out other girls in the meantime. Buying 'em flowers and candy and shit. Didn't look like you loved me then."

Donnie laughed. "You sound a lil' jealous, Ma. I only took out those other broads to help me pass the time. I had to do something to take my mind off of you. You were too busy crying over that bastard and shit."

"Now who sounds jealous?"

"I admit it. I was jealous of him. Only because I knew that he didn't deserve you. I didn't know he was cheating on you, but I knew he wasn't giving you the time and attention you needed. You're like a flower baby. You need careful attention, love and nurturing in order to grow and flourish. Everything you need is right here with me baby. I got you"

"You got me, D?"

"Yep. You and me gon' roll til' the wheels fall off."

Donnie opened the blinds to let the moonlight in. It casted a soft glow over Symone's skin. A smile spread across her face when she looked up to see Donnie watching her. She lifted her arms and motioned for her to come to her and get back into bed. Symone drifted off into a deep sleep. Donnie got up and checked her phone. She had a picture message of a woman lying in bed, naked. It was sent ten minutes ago.

"*Wet and waiting*," the message stated.

"On my way," Donnie quickly replied.

Without leaving a note or even a goodbye kiss, Donnie left. As soon as she crossed the threshold of the other woman's house, her clothes were off and she was knee deep in pussy. They both came so hard they fell asleep. Late in the midnight hour, another wave of arousal coursed through Donnie's body and she made love to Charmaine until the sun came up.

# Changing Seasons

November came in with a gust of cold, rushing wind and the days flew past like leaves in the breeze, changing the weather overnight. Before anyone realized, half of the month had gone and in a few short weeks, Thanksgiving would be upon them. The weather wasn't the only thing that had changed in Atlanta. The friendship between Symone, Jynx and Devine had also. Ever since Symone had hooked up with Donnie, she was distant from her friends. Their Sunday breakfast meetings had ceased, and every time Jynx or Devine called Symone, she was too busy to talk. Symone never seemed to answer her phone anymore. Donnie always had it. As a counselor, Jynx knew the signs.

Jynx didn't like Donnie at all. Not because she was a lesbian, but there was something about her that rubbed her the wrong way. The few times they'd all gotten together had not gone over well. Jynx tried talking to Symone about her feelings but her friend wasn't trying to hear it. She didn't like having serious conversations over the phone. But the only place she seemed to be able to reach Symone was at her desk at the station. First, Symone laughed it off, but then she got angry.

"I'm sick and tired of you and Devine all up in my business. Why can't the two of you just be cool that I'm finally happy? Maybe if you got a man, and a relationship of your own, then you wouldn't be all up in mine."

"Wow. You really went there, didn't you? I have a man. A real one and he comes with equipment straight from the manufacturer. Puh-lease, you wish you had it this good. So I tell you what, you don't have to worry about me being in your business now or ever!"

After that, Jynx hung up the phone and they hadn't spoken since then. That was almost two weeks ago. Jynx missed her friend but wasn't going to kiss her ass just to make things right. Everybody who knew Donnie knew that she was bad news. Hopefully, Symone would come to her senses before it was too late. Jynx picked up her cell phone to check a text message. She looked at the screen and saw that it was from Keyon. She opened up the message and saw that he asked her to call him so she did.

"What's up, dude?" she asked.

"Not much. Just sitting here in the office, contemplating my next move, laughing at Devine's crazy ass. Yo' boy is wild."

"You didn't know? Is he with you? What you guys got going on?"

"Nah, he not up here for me, he came to visit a cat who works up here in the music library. He just stopped in to check on me. Trying to get me to buy his broke ass dinner tonight."

"He knows I'm on a fixed income, Jynx!" Devine yelled over Keyon's shoulder into the phone. She laughed on the other end.

"Anyway, that's really not such a bad idea. Why don't you two come by the house? There's something that I've been meaning to show you. I'll cook something for us to eat and we can talk afterwards. Y'all game?" Keyon proposed.

"Now you know I will never turn down a free meal," Devine remarked.

"I'm in. I have a few errands to run but I'll come right after," Jynx said.

"Thanks. See ya' soon."

She grabbed her rose colored Balenciaga handbag, her shades and car keys and headed out. Keyon was not just her cousin. He was more like the brother she never had. His happiness and well-being meant as much to her as her own, and so did Devine's. *It used to be the same way with Symone until she got with that she-male,* Jynx thought, pissed off.

"No negative thoughts allowed. Symone is grown. She has her life and I have mine. And I'm going to concentrate on myself. Just like my girl, Fantasia. Sang it Fanny!" Jynx said out loud as she turned up the volume on Fantasia Barrino's latest hit *'Doing Me'*.

Jynx cracked her window to let a little air in and started singing along with the track, sounding like a cat on a hot tin roof.

A few hours later Jynx pulled up in front of Keyon's house and was preparing to get out when her phone rang. Jill Scott starting singing *'Is It the Way He Loves Me'* as the ring tone let Jynx know that Jonathan was calling. Smiling, she answered the phone.

"Hey you," she said

"Hey, babe. How are you?" he replied.

"I'm good. I was just thinking about you."

"Oh, really now? And what were you thinking?"

"Mmm, I can show you better than I can tell you," she said seductively.

"Awe, shit. I'm on my way over right now then."

After she finished laughing she said, "I would love to see you right now but I'm at Keyon's. I just pulled up. Me and Devine are having dinner with him tonight."

"Cool. I'm still at the office anyway. Will I see you tonight?"

"Of course. I'll text you as soon as I leave here. You can come by my place. We can watch a movie," she offered.

"Bet! I'll bring the popcorn."

"You do that. And Jonathan, bring something else."

"What?" he asked.

"Your toothbrush." And with that, she hung up the phone.

She wasn't letting that fine specimen out of her sight tonight. She got out of the car and went inside the house to find

Keyon and Devine in the kitchen, cooking and talking.

"I didn't know you were here, D," she said to Devine, hugging him and kissing him on the cheek. "I didn't see your car outside."

"My car is at the house, I rode over with Keyon. He was nice enough to follow me home so I could drop Felicity off. She needs her rest you know?"

"Boy, you so silly. What made you name your car Felicity of all things?"

"You know how much he loved that show, Jynx. He wanted to be Keri Russell," Keyon put in.

"Hell that bitch is ca-yute. Can you blame me?"

The friends laughed and talked about everything from their favorite television shows of the past to all the expensive hairpieces Cha-Cha and Devine had invested in over the years. Keyon almost choked on his food when Devine told them that the reason he moved into a three-bedroom house was so he could have a room for his wig heads. They were all doubled over with laughter. When they all settled down, Jynx asked Devine about his plans for Thanksgiving.

"I'm eating where ever you two are," Devine remarked.

"Cool beans. We're eating here for dinner. Everyone is coming over." Keyon folded his napkin in his plate, sitting back in his chair. The room had gone quiet.

"Has anyone heard from her?" Devine asked, breaking the silence. Keyon shook his head no and Jynx told them what happened the last time she spoke with her.

"I just can't believe that she would believe some video over you. Especially knowing how technology is these days. People can do almost anything now with a computer," she added.

"Well, that's why I invited the two of you over here. I want to show you something and then we can talk about it afterwards." Keyon got up from the table.

The three of them went to Keyon's studio. He grabbed the DVD remote and pressed play. He watched the sex tape every day. The more he watched it, the more desire built up inside of him for the unknown woman who had captivated him in such a way that he was willing to risk five years with Symone for another night with her. Something told him that she needed him. And when he found her, he would tell her just how much he really needed her.

Keyon didn't even have to watch the video. Every second of that video was embedded in his membranes. He knew every curve of her body, the octave of every moan that passed her lips, the look on her face when she came, like she was coming for the first time. He remembered the pleasure on her face when he came inside her. If he only he could remember that night...

"Damn, Keyon! You were working that bitch's pussy like a pro. I got a lil' moist watching you in action. Shit!" Devine joked.

"She's not a bitch!" Keyon yelled angrily.

"Whoa, cousin. You know how Devine is. He didn't mean any harm. Where is all this anger coming from?" Jynx asked softly.

"That's just it, J. I don't know. I get angry at myself for always defending this girl when she is part of the reason that me and Symone are no longer together. And then I get angry because I feel..." his voice faded.

"You feel what, Keyon?"

"I feel like I'm connected to this girl, Jynx. Like I, like I'm in love with her. And before you and Devine start telling me how crazy I sound, I already know. What's wrong with me, cuz?"

"Keyon, you're not crazy. I totally understand where you're coming from. There's no way to explain it, you simply feel the way that you do. But um, I'm not trying to rub salt in your wounds but, I see why Symone left."

"You saw it too, huh?" Keyon asked.

"Saw what?" Devine questioned.

"Yes. I think she saw it, too."

141

"Who is she and what did she see?" Devine asked agitated.

"That's what I said myself. Hell, I would have left me, too," Keyon added.

"I know you mofo's hear me. Who is she and what in the hell did she see?"

Jynx put him out of his misery. "Symone, D. *She* is Symone and what I believe she saw was her man making love very thoroughly to another woman. So much so, that his dick never left her pussy. Not even when he rolled over. Now that's some good pussy."

"Oh. Yeah, I saw that. Well Keyon, what you gon' do? At first when I heard about the tape, I didn't think that it was you. But after seeing it, it's most definitely you. So how are you planning on getting Symone back? Isn't that why you called us over? To help you?"

"We got your back, cousin. We are here to help," Jynx added.

"Yes, I need you all's help, but not to get Symone back. I want you two to help me find her," he said, pointing at the screen."

And with that, the three of them began to formulate a plan.

• • • • • • • • • • • • • • • • •

With the sudden disappearance of Morgan, Donnie's finances fell off drastically. It had been almost two months since her last car payment, and the finance company was threatening to repossess it. She'd been calling Morgan for a couple of weeks but the phone always went to voicemail. Donnie had left so many messages that her mailbox was full. Donnie made the August payment on her own when she received her final paycheck from her job, but she missed September and October. In a few days, the November payment would be due and then she would really be in trouble.

Right now, she was between jobs and didn't have the

$820 to give to Luxor Auto Credit. Luckily, she knew someone who did. She pretended like she was ending a phone call when Symone walked into the room and got a sad look on her face.

"Yes, I understand. Well, thank you for your assistance anyway."

"Hey my love, why the sad face?" Symone asked, sitting in her girlfriend's lap.

"That was the bank. Apparently, the investigation they started on my account for that identity theft mess is still on going. She said it could take another forty-five days to resolve the issue."

"Well, I know that sucks but it's no reason to have a long face."

"I wouldn't be tripping if my car payment wasn't affected by this. Because of this bullshit, my car payment is almost three months behind and they're going to take it."

"Why didn't you tell me this before?"

"Because babe, I don't want to burden you with my mess. I'll figure it out. Hell, losing a car ain't shit. The worst that can happen is that it'll be on my credit. They may be able to take that car, but at least they can't take you," Donnie said in a syrupy sweet voice.

"Baby, you're always thinking of others instead of yourself. That's why you're so blessed. Don't worry about your car note. I'll take care of it until the bank fixes your issues."

"Babe, you ain't gotta do all that. I'm supposed to be taking care of you, not the other way around."

"Now see, that's where you're wrong. We're supposed to be taking care of each other."

"Damn girl, I love you so much."

Symone smiled. "I love you, too."

Donnie had gotten exactly what she wanted. Symone turned on the television and Channel 3 Action News was covering a story regarding a fire in S.W. Atlanta. When they showed the house, Donnie recognized it immediately.

"Yo, turn that up. That's my home girl Nina's house."

*"A man was arrested after an investigation into a suspicious house fire on Cascade Terrace that happened in the early morning hours almost two weeks ago, according to the Atlanta Fire Department. James Hudson, 34, was arrested for 3rd degree arson and 2nd degree murder after the body of his former lover was found inside of her torched home. According to investigators, Mr. Hudson was angry that Ms. Carter was allegedly having an affair. We'll have more on this story and information unfolds. Back to you, Bill."*

"How did you know her, babe?" Symone asked, rubbing Donnie's back.

*Well, that explains why she never returned any of my calls. Damn, now who's going to pay my car insurance?* "We used to work together," Donnie lied.

"Wow. That's unfortunate what happened to her," Symone sympathized. Donnie couldn't have agreed more.

• • • • • • • • • • • • • • • • • •

It may have taken a while, but Kimmy Bradshaw finished organizing all of the police reports on her desk, and this time she managed to enter them all into the computer. Sergeant Blair would finally be able to follow up with the victims, and maybe, just maybe, offer them some sort of resolution. While she was entering the information into the system, she did notice that the most recent reports were from women who said they were either lesbian or bi-sexual. She would have to tell Sarge that when she saw him. That is, if she even remembered.

• • • • • • • • • • • • • • • • • •

Watson McCoy, private investigator, was one of the best in the business. Watson believed that he could find anything and anyone. He could have unearthed the body of Jimmy Hoffa if they had put him on the case. Until this case, he had had a 100% success rate. Whoever Domynique Segar was, she didn't want to be found. He uncovered many facts about her, but she cut herself completely off from any friends she may have had and all of her family members.

Watson saw the sex tape. To help him, he made some still photos so that he could examine her closely. Only when he got the photos developed, did Watson pay attention to a tattoo on the girl's left shoulder. It was a birth date and he was going to use that to help track her down.

# A Decent Proposal

Jynx was more than satisfied. It had been a long time since she woke up feeling that good. She stretched and rolled over towards her night stand, but a strong arm slid under her waist and pulled her back into the curve of his body.

"Not so fast. Get back here, Sexy. It's way too early for you to be getting out of bed."

"I wasn't. Just wanted to give you space so you could sleep better. I didn't know you were awake."

"I sleep better with you next to me. I don't know why you have this monstrosity anyway," he said, referring to the California king-sized bed.

"I got this bed because I knew one day I would have someone to share it with."

"So, you wanna share a bed with me, huh?" Jonathan asked.

"I do. I'm not saying that you have to move in with me, but I would love to have more mornings where I can wake up in your arms."

"Jynx," he began seriously. "As appealing as that sounds, I'm going to have to pass."

"Wh- what?" she asked incredulously.

"You heard me. I'm gonna have to pass," Jonathan repeated, getting out of the bed and leaving the room.

Jynx didn't know whether to scream or cry or both. Her mind was reeling. How could she go from waking up on cloud nine to landing in the dirt? Hot tears burned the corners of her eyes and threatened to spill over. This wasn't the end of their relationship, was it? He just didn't want to be spending the night. That's all he meant, right?

Jonathan returned to the room carrying a silver-plated breakfast tray, with juice, fresh melon, scrambled eggs and bacon for two. He set the tray down on the bistro table on the balcony adjacent to her bedroom. Jynx was so discombobulated by his rejection that she didn't even notice what was happening. He walked over to her and handed her the black silk Kimono that was draped over her armchair. He escorted her to the table and the two of them ate breakfast in the warm morning sunlight.

Jonathan stared at Jynx. It wasn't his intention to make her cry. Any man would have jumped at what she offered. But he wasn't just any man. Moreover, she wasn't just any woman. He didn't want a few nights at her place and a few nights at his. He wanted the luxury, the honor, of waking up with her every day, and there only one way to accomplish that.

"Babe, you know how you were telling me that you don't just accept any client? How you interview them kinda to see if they will benefit from your services?"

She nodded yes.

"And like, when you look for a job, it doesn't take years of interviews to decide if you're the right person for the position. A person may interview twice, maybe even three times for a job before he decides to hire someone."

"Jonathan, what's with all the interview talk? Are you leaving M.O.S.? I mean, what gives?"

"What I'm trying to say is, it doesn't take forever to know if something is right or not. I knew from the first moment I laid eyes on you in Keyon's office that you were the woman I wanted to spend the rest of my life with. And babe, as much as I wanted to say we can start sleeping over at one another's houses, I knew I needed more than that from you."

"So, what are you trying to say, Jonathan?" Jynx asked with tears in her eyes, praying it was what she was thinking.

Jonathan picked up the stereo remote and pressed play.

That was yet another thing, Jynx didn't pay attention to. Music filled the room while the background singers sang;

*Couldn't we be, be happily ever after?*
*We could be strong together for so long*
*Couldn't we be, be happily ever after?*
*Leavin' you never 'til forever's gone*

"I'm not trying to say it my love, I'm saying it," as he got down on one knee. "Jynx Ja'Lynn Jacobi, will you do me the honors of being my wife and putting me out of my misery?"

"Yes!" she shouted happily, jumping into his arms.

He picked her up and carried her to the bed and kissed her passionately. She returned the kiss as her hands explored his body. His chest flexed under her fingers and she giggled.

"This is the only eating that needs to be done in this bed." Jonathan eased slowly into her warm, pink center with his mouth. His tongue made lazy circles around her pearl tongue before he started sucking on it and fingering her. Jynx began to convulse as a result of Jonathans skillfulness. When he came up for air, he entered her slowly and they began a slow grind until they picked up speed. He slid in and out of her wetness, over and over until the friction began to burn her insides and she was on the verge of climaxing. Her eyes crossed as the first wave of tingling coursed through her body.

Jonathan lay on his side and laid Jynx on her side in front of him and lifted her leg. She grinded her hips into the mattress and pushed her ass back to greet his big dick at the same time. He rubbed her clitoris and kissed on her neck, his own release just seconds from coming. His butt cheeks clenched as he pounded into her wet snatch. She moaned, "I'm coming" and the two of them erupted together.

Jynx smiled from ear to ear as she cuddled with her fiancé. The sun was shining brightly through her window. She was blissfully happy. The diamond on her finger was impeccable. Before she dozed off with him for a morning nap, she thought about how blessed she was to meet such a wonderful guy. Now she understood where Keyon was coming from. There may be something more to his feelings for the video vixen than she had first imagined. She would talk to him about it later. Right now, she was going to rest in her future husband's arms. Since he liked it, he went and put a ring on it.

•••••••••••••••••

"Oh. Ooh. Oh, yes. Mmm. That's how I like it, Daddy. I'm cum-ming," Charmaine sang, floating back down to Earth after that mind-blowing orgasm. "I love waking up with my clit in your mouth, baby. We make love more now that we live apart than we did when we lived together."

"I know. That's because we were getting too comfortable with one another. We took each other for granted. Didn't appreciate the good love we had right in our own home. Now that we live apart, we are able to see and appreciate each other more and we make the best of our time together."

"Whatever it is, I like it. I thought that we were over."

"We can never be over. You know I can never get enough of you."

"I know that. I feel the same way."

"Real talk, Char. If I can't have you, nobody can."

"I'm yours and you're mine. Always."

"Damn skippy. Now spread them thick legs for Daddy and let me finish what I started," Donnie said to Charmaine, and the two made love for the rest of the morning.

•••••••••••••••••

The wax from the burned out candles ran down the side of the table, but cooled before hitting the floor, looking like icicles. The steak and baked potato looked dehydrated. Wilted iceberg lettuce, brown apple chunks and stiff salad dressing made up the once delicious looking salad. Both plates sat on the table, untouched. The bottle of wine sat in a bucket of warm water, which used to be ice. What was supposed to be a romantic dinner turned out to be a flop.

Symone didn't understand. Donnie called the night before and said she was on her way home but she never made it. This wasn't like her. She would come in really late or very early, depending, but Symone expected that because her girlfriend picked up some extra gigs bouncing at a few nightclubs. Even though she worked odd hours she always made it home. Until last night.

She sent several text messages; all went unanswered, and had called well over twenty- five times. The phone went straight to voice mail. Worry settled in. Had a fight broken out at a club? Did she get caught in the mix? Was she hurt? It drove her crazy not knowing. None of the area hospitals treated a Donita Stone. As much as she didn't want to, Symone picked up the phone to call Damian, Donnie's brother, to see if he heard from his sister. She dialed the number and waited for him to pick up. Instead of the deep voice she expected to hear, she heard a soft, sweet one just waking up from a good sleep.

"Hello," Stephanie, Damian's girlfriend asked groggily.

"Good morning, Stephanie. I'm sorry to wake you. This is Symone, Donnie's girlfriend. She didn't make it home last night and I got kinda worried. May I please speak with her?"

"Donnie didn't sleep here last night, Symone."

"Oh my goodness. God, I hope she's okay."

"Take it from me," Stephanie began, "Donnie is okay. She's probably laid up at the next bitch house. If I were you, I'd cut my losses now before she uses you up and hangs you out to dry like she did Charmaine."

"Well, you're not me, are you? I didn't call seeking unsolicited relationship advice. I just wanted to know if you all had seen her," she said in a huff.

"Look," Stephanie said softly, "I'm not trying to be all up in yours. But if you've been messing with Donnie a lil while then I'm sure she told you about her exes? I'm sure she failed to mention that she was in a relationship with a crazy ass bitch who tried to slice my face. I'm telling you, that child ain't wrapped too tight."

Stunned by that information, Symone quietly said, "No, she didn't tell me that."

"Humph, she always seems to leave that part out. But like I said before, I ain't tryna tell you what to do but you need to be careful."

Symone listened to Stephanie bashing Donnie for four or five more minutes before ending the call. *Donnie was right*, she thought. *Shit, no matter how much a person changed, some people were always going to hold the past against them.* It didn't matter what anyone else thought, Symone believed in Donnie and the love they shared. Donnie was loving, kind, considerate and most importantly, faithful, the main thing that Keyon was not. She wasn't going to let anyone plant a seed of distrust in her. She was not going to accuse her of doing anything that she didn't witness herself.

Donnie had many friends and probably just got drunk and passed out with one of them. She would be home. Of that, Symone was sure. She grabbed her keys and went to get her hands and feet done. Whatever time Donnie came home, she would be waiting like the pretty partner she was, wearing nothing more than the skin God gave her.

# Forever Yours, Unfaithfully…

It took three, very long, stressful days for Donnie to come home. Symone went the entire weekend without one bit of communication from her girlfriend. Lord knows how many texts she sent. She called so much that she stopped counting after 217 calls. And let's not forget the tears. She cried so much she could have filled two, five-gallon water jugs, leaving her eyes red and puffy. Keyon never stayed out all night. If he was going to be late he would always call *and* text. But Donnie wasn't Keyon, and every day, Symone was beginning to see that.

It was six in the morning when Symone heard the key in the lock. She thought that she heard someone at the door a few times before, only to end up looking foolish after she ran to the door, swinging it open, to find no one standing there. Instead of repeating that walk of shame, she continued to lie on the sofa, where she had been for the past two days. Thirty seconds later, her eyelids flew back and she jumped up, covering her ears as the alarm blared loudly, waking everyone within a five block radius. Symone ran over to the keypad and punched in the code, silencing the electronic menace.

"What the fuck is that?" Donnie yelled.

"It's an intrusion alarm. A security system…" Symone began sarcastically before being interrupted.

"I know what the fuck it is. What's it doing here?"

"I had it installed for security and protection."

"I don't know who in da hell you think you talking to but your ass can miss me with all the slick shit. When you get this joint and why?"

"It was installed Saturday, and like I said before, I had it installed for security and protection."

"You ain't got no more times to disrespect me, Symone. I'm trying to be cool here."

"Disrespect you? You have got to be kidding me! You're the disrespectful one! Staying out for three days, no calling or texting. You weren't worried about me when you were out laying up with the next bitch! Now, where were you?"

"What? Get the fuck out of here! I've been working Symone. Working! So that I could get money to pay you back for everything that you've done for me."

"Yeah, right. I called all the clubs that you were supposedly 'working' at and no one has seen or heard from you."

"Oh, so you checking up on me now, Symone? You don't trust me? For your information, I bounce at more places than just those hole-in-the-wall-clubs. Here, see for yourself if you don't believe me," Donnie said, throwing an envelope at Symone.

Reluctantly, Symone picked up the envelope that held over three thousand dollars cash and a thank you note from a Masonic group in Tennessee thanking Donnie for her services. The letter also invited her back to serve as head of security at the same time next year.

"But this still doesn't explain why you didn't call or text me back?"

Donnie walked over to Symone and backhanded her so hard she flew into the entertainment cabinet.

"I ain't that nigga Keyon. You can't talk to me just any kind of way and you gon' learn today not to question me."

Symone got up off the floor. "Is this why you chased me? Boxing practice?" she screamed.

"Bitch I don't chase my liquor, why would I chase you?"

"Whatever, Donnie. You fuck up, but I'm the one who suffers. What is it about me that makes you so angry?" she said tearfully.

Softening, Donnie replied, "baby, it's not you, it's me. You know I love you. You believe that don't you?"

"Yes, but…"

"No buts. You love me and I love you. I'm not going to let my anger or my fists get the best of me again. I don't wanna lose you. You're all I need in my life."

What Donnie really needed was Symone's financial support. When Donnie first started listening to Symone's radio show, all she used to talk about was how women are supposed to treat men in relationships. The picture she painted for Donnie was one of a subservient, docile woman who paid for everything and that is the woman that Donnie wanted to meet and be with. She hadn't planned on meeting Ms. Independent, but she was going to break her of that shit one way or the other.

"I'm sorry. I know it's my fault you get angry. I never should've doubted you."

"It's all good. I love you. Come on over here and give me a proper greeting. Stop being so standoffish."

Symone closed the few feet of space that separated her and Donnie. She was met with open arms and a passionate kiss that let her know she was missed. But being hit again still nagged at her that wouldn't allow her to surrender to the passion Donnie tried to evoke.

"Damn girl, I missed these sexy lips," Donnie said between kisses.

"Both sets?" Symone asked seductively.

"Both sets," she answered as she proceeded to savor every inch of her girlfriend's body.

Her lips were so soft on Symone's skin. The way they gently brushed her forehead sent chills down her back. Donnie smelled so good to Symone. Curve for Men was her cologne of choice even though Symone bought her better and more expensive brands. Cologne and Donnie's own natural scent turned Symone on the most. Her breath caught in her throat when Donnie's hot tongue snaked down her neck and back up to that small indentation behind her ears. That was Symone's spot.

155

Her clit began to throb. Donnie was making love to that spot and Symone's body started to go crazy with need. With one hand, Donnie slowly began to knead her lovers' breasts through her sheer camisole. Her nipples hardened. Donnie stopped kissing her long enough to remove Symone's top and unhook her bra. Her large D cup breasts spilled out and Donnie's hot mouth covered one of Symone's nipples and she began licking it uncontrollably. Her tongue flicked the other nipple playfully causing the heat at Symone's core to intensify.

Donnie walked her backward toward the bedroom. Once Symone's legs touched the edge of the bed Donnie turned her around to face the bed and slowly traveled the length of Symone's torso until her thumbs locked in the elastic of the shorts she was wearing. She slid them down over her hips. Donnie's lips assaulted Symone's back, sending kisses down her spine. Her long fingers tickled Symone's pussy like a pianist strokes the ivory keys of a piano. Symone grinded her ass hard against Donnie's pelvis, trying to feel for her hard bulge, forgetting for a moment that she was a woman. Instead, her ass found Donnie's G-spot and she responded by vigorously pumping Symone's ass while grasping hold to her. Symone knew by Donnie's erratic breathing that she was getting ready to come. While her bucking continued, she lifted one of Symone's legs on the bed and slid her fingers in her pussy deeper. In and out. Round and round.

"Damn baby, you're so fucking wet."

"That's what you do to me, Daddy."

The room was quiet with the exception of their groans. Donnie dropped to her knees and bit her girl's bottom. Her hands spread Symone's cheeks apart, and her tongue circled her asshole before she made it stiff and slid it in. Symone knees buckled from the sensation. Donnie tongue fucked her ass and fingered her pussy at the same time. Sweet, creamy cum ran down the inside of Symone's thighs and on Donnie's hand.

Removing her tongue from one hole, she quickly slid it into the other and reversed positions. She sucked her pussy and fingered her asshole. This time, Symone collapsed, lying face down on the bed, and gyrated the mattress as if Donnie was under her. Just feeling her lips wrapped around her clit like gave Symone a head rush. Getting off her knees, Donnie walked across the room, away from Symone who whimpered in protest.

"Oh don't worry sweetheart, Daddy got something he know you gon' like."

Still lying on her stomach, Symone felt the bed shift under Donnie's weight and she spread her legs apart. Donnie's fingers entered her pussy briefly, distributing wetness to her back door. In one swift movement, Symone felt her slide a thick, long dildo inside her pussy and a small vibrating bullet into her ass. She fucked her pussy like a pro. Finding all the spots that every man before her had missed.

"Turn over," Donnie instructed. Symone obeyed.

Her voice was deep and full of passion. She wanted to go deeper in her girlfriend's cavern than she had been before. In the missionary position she loved Symone right. Her mouth found her breasts again and caused more pressure to build in her center. She had both of her legs straight up in the air. Their skin made slapping noises. Her grip tightened on her legs. She banged the other woman's pussy. Her legs fell apart in a spilt. Donnie rubbed her clit. Her moans deepened. Symone started to whimper. The dick stroked her insides. The two women kissed passionately. Donnie laid the vibrator on Symone's engorged clit. She started to cum again. She heard her name pass through Donnie's lips in a guttural sound, sounding like a wounded wild animal. Symone found her own release and she grabbed Donnie's ass, pulling her in to the hilt of her love. The two women had crossed over to the other side.

"I love you," Symone said softly.

"I love you, too," Donnie replied.

Their lovemaking was so intense that they could have made a baby if it were possible. Donnie gathered Symone in her arms and pulled her into the mold of her body. Symone lay there, spooning with her girlfriend, exhausted from the orgasms, and happy that her lover was home. As she dozed off, she just knew that when she woke up they would do this all over again. How wrong she was.

Symone woke up alone. But instead of lying in bed mad at the world that Donnie abandoned her again, she thought she'd make the most of her day and clean house. Donnie had left a note stating that she was going to buy a new phone and that she'd pick up dinner on the way back home. *The least I can do is clean the house and make it nice for her,* she thought.

As usual, Donnie hadn't put any of her things away, leaving her duffle bag at the door. Since she'd moved in, Symone felt like she was more of a maid than a girlfriend at times. Keyon was meticulous and loved things in order. *There I go thinking about him again.* She picked up the bag and dumped the clothes on the floor. Something fell out landing in a soft thud. There were dirty boxer briefs in the midst of the jeans and shirts. One pair even had a skid mark in the seat.

"Damn, she's nasty like a trifling ass, dude," Symone mumbled out loud.

Dirty socks, a couple of white T-shirts and a couple of sports bras were the last of the clothes. She sorted all of the clothes and then remembered she forgot to check the pockets. She reached into the bag and felt inside a dress shirt pocket, finding a business card and a stick of gum. One of the pairs of jeans held an empty condom wrapper, a few stray rose petals and the skimpiest pair of thongs she had ever seen. Symone flew off the handle.

"What the fuck is this shit? She brought another bitches shit into my house?" *Fuck! Stephanie was right. She was out fucking the next bitch. Her ass ain't no different than a nigga. First Keyon and now her. It's cool, though. I got something for her ass.* "She got me fucked up!" Symone yelled as she gathered the rest of the bags contents off of the floor. She took a step and her foot knocked something across the floor. It lodged under a shelf. Symone crouched down and brushed her hand under the shelf and then a flat, dusty object materialized. It was Donnie's iPhone that she claimed to have lost. She powered it up long enough to see some pictures of some bitches pussy and read some very explicit text messages. Enraged, Symone found a hammer and smashed the phone to bits, putting it in the trash compactor and sending it out with the day's garbage, but not before forwarding the pictures and messages to her private email account.

Symone couldn't believe she had trusted Donnie. She promised that she'd never treat her badly or cheat on her. All lies. Fucking with a woman was no different than fucking with a man. Symone grabbed her purse to leave, but when she went to kitchen for her keys, they were gone. She looked in her purse to get the spare out of her wallet and noticed that it was gone also. Donnie had taken it. Stuck at home and pissed off, Symone decided that she wasn't going to sit and cry. If Donnie wanted to play, Symone was down. Game on.

• • • • • • • • • • • • • • • • •

Charmaine enjoyed the time in Vegas with Donnie immensely even though she foot the bill. But paying for the trip now would mean separation for Donnie and Symone later. Donnie hadn't changed so Charmaine counted on her being the same nasty slob she was when they lived together and leave her things lying around. On their way to Vegas, when they were waiting to board the plane Donnie kept looking at her phone, not answering for whoever was incessantly calling. Then she got up and went to the bathroom. When she returned, she didn't have the phone.

Before they boarded, Charmaine went to the bathroom and called her lying lovers phone. On the wall nearby, the trashcan hummed. Reluctantly, Charmaine got the device out, and hid it in the bottom of her carry-on. Charmaine was sure that Donnie was going to tell Symone that she had lost it. She would make sure that Miss Symone had something to look at when Donnie got back to Georgia. She was going to break up Donnie's happy home and when Symone put her out, she would have no choice but to come crawling back to Charmaine. And Charmaine would be waiting with open arms.

# Who's Fooling Who?...

Jynx, Cha-Cha and Devine sat in the waiting room of Cha-Cha's doctor's office waiting for her to get the stitches removed from her hand. The trio had been hanging tough since Jynx and Symone were now on the outs. It went without saying that all of them missed their friend but no one was going to beg her to hang out with them. They were talking about everything under the sun when a handsome doctor walked into the room and waved at the group as he passed them. Devine gasped and leaned back in his seat like he was swooning, fanning himself with his left hand. "Lions and tigers and bears, oh my. Is that your doctor? I'm feeling weak now. You think he can squeeze in me, I mean, squeeze me in?"

Cha-Cha laughed but shook her head. "Chile, I wish that was my doctor. That's his partner though, Dr. Broadhead. And judging by the way he walks, I concur." The three friends broke out in laughter. A few more doctors came in and went to the back. All of them were good looking as well.

"It's raining men up in here. No wonder you like coming."

"Ms. Rodriguez, Doctor Lashio will see you now," the nurse said from behind the counter.

Cha-Cha got up to walk away back but stopped short. "The only thing that would make my doctor better is if his first name was Phil." With that, she sauntered away, leaving the nurse red-faced and embarrassed, Jynx confused, and Devine doubled over in laughter.

"I don't get it. Phil?" Jynx asked. Her forehead creased in confusion.

Devine's laughter subsided. "Yes, dear heart. Then his doctors' name would be Phil Lashio. Felatio. Get it now?"

"Ugh, you two get on my nerves," she said, and they both broke out into another round of laughter.

After catching his breath, Devine asked Jynx if she had spoken to Symone recently. She told him that she hadn't.

"I haven't either, but the other day I saw her looking like a hot ghetto mess, wearing a scarf and some Gucci knock off shades. She was trying to duck and dodge so I wouldn't see her but honey, you gotta know that these beautiful browns right here don't miss a thing," he finished, pointing at his eyes.

"Are you sure it was her?" Jynx asked incredulously. "She never leaves her house unless she's dressed to impress.

"Girl, I'm sure. It was her ass. And get this; word on the street is that not only is Donnie a lying cheat, she's kicking Symone's ass, too."

"Get the hell out of here? Donnie beats Symone? The Symone I knew wouldn't stand for that. She'd scratch that bitches eyes out," Jynx said angrily.

"Knew being the operative word. She's not the same."

"I should call her. See how she's doing."

"Go right ahead," Devine said. "As soon as I heard what was going on I called her. That heifer answered the phone and when she heard my voice the trick hung up on me. Then she called back claiming it was a dropped call," Devine finished, getting angry all over again.

"Well, that could have been the case. You know how cell phones are these days," Jynx attempted to defend Symone.

"What the fuck ever. That would fly if I hadn't called the trick on her *work* phone."

"Boi stop!" Jynx dialed Symone's number. "Sshhh, it's ringing. Hey Symone, it's Jynx. I was just calling to see how you were doing." The friends exchanged formalities and small talk. Jynx told her about her man and other things that were going on with her and the family. "Symone, I just want you to know that no matter who you're with, Devine, Cha-cha and I are here for you. We love you. Symone? Can you hear me?"

"I told you she would hang up," Devine whispered.

"Symone?" Jynx heard sniffles on the other end. Symone was crying.

"I'm here, Jynx. Thank you. I love you guys, too."

"We still meet at the Flying Biscuit on Saturday's. You should come. We'd love to see you. Oh and Donnie too if you'd like to bring her."

"That sounds nice. I'll ask Donnie if I can come,' Symone said. "Look, she's getting out of the shower, I gotta go. Thanks for calling," and hung up.

"What did she say? I'm surprised she answered."

"I was too, Devine. She said she would try to come if Donnie let her."

"What the fuck! If Donnie let her? Oh my fucking gosh. Definitely not the same person we once knew."

They chatted for another few minutes until Cha-cha came out. Over lunch, they filled her in about the phone conversation. It was obvious that Symone was changing, and not for the better. They feared she had been turned out to the point of no return.

• • • • • • • • • • • • • • • • •

A frustrated Kimmy Bradshaw sat at her desk staring at the crazy cases that were still open. The cases all had a common denominator; all of the victims were lesbian or bi-sexual and all had messed with someone named, Dee, Donnie or Stone. Unfortunately, none of the victims were very cooperative when it came to identifying their lover. She was stumped. Until she got a call from Cha-cha earlier. In her frustration she told her friend about a few of the cases and accidentally mentioned a name associated with a case.

"Stone?" Cha-cha asked. "Like Donnie Stone?"

"What the hell? Donnie Stone is one name? I thought it

was three different people. Damn, why didn't I figure that out a long time ago?" She typed the name in her system. "Son of a bitch. Hey Diva, I gotta go. I need to call my boss." Kimmy hit speed dial on her cell phone. "Boss man, I have a name *and* an address. I'll text it to you. Let's do this."

● ● ● ● ● ● ● ● ● ● ● ● ● ● ● ● ●

The Monday before Thanksgiving proved to be a beautiful day in Atlanta. This would be the first year Charmaine had a guest in her home for the holiday and she was very excited. After she completed some self-assigned chores, she decided to kick back and watch a little closed circuit television. It was going to be a very good day indeed.

● ● ● ● ● ● ● ● ● ● ● ● ● ● ● ● ●

One of Donnie's homeboys was having a pre-Thanksgiving gathering Tuesday evening and she didn't want to come empty handed. This dude was known to hob knob with Atlanta's elite and Donnie wanted to get in where she fit in. She wanted to bring some of Symone's stuffed peppers to impress him. But getting Symone to make enough for her to take to dude's party *and* to her own potluck at work was going to be a task. Symone was still mad at her about staying out all those days and the fight. If Donnie wanted Symone to do anything for her, she was going to have to kiss her ass.

● ● ● ● ● ● ● ● ● ● ● ● ● ● ● ● ●

As much as Symone wanted to forgive Donnie she just couldn't. She couldn't ignore the evidence that she found. Having been with Donnie a few months Symone was learning how selfish and self-centered the woman really was. Her lover was a world-class liar, cheater and abuser. Symone was going to make her pay for hurting her. Donnie had been hinting around for Symone to prepare her Granny's famous stuffed peppers for her but she had refused. However, Symone decided that she was going to make them and add a little something special to the recipe.

She pulled out her grandmother's recipe and once she had most of the mechanics done with the peppers she began working on the sauce. After adding all the ingredients that Grandma Morrow's recipe called for, she added a few of her own; three tablespoons of phlegm she managed to cough up, two turds she squeezed out right before coming into the kitchen and a quarter cup of blood that slowly dripped from her bleeding pussy as she sat, having a bowel movement on the toilet. With gloved hands, she added the ingredients to the recipe.

Pleased with the way the mixture appeared, Symone stuffed the peppers, sprinkled them with cheese and placed them in the oven to bake. An hour later she pulled them out of the oven, and to the naked eye, they looked and smelled delicious. She made quick work of cleaning the kitchen and went lie down to finish some work for her show. With a smile on her face, waited for her cheating lover to return to claim her culinary prize.

● ● ● ● ● ● ● ● ● ● ● ● ● ● ● ● ●

When the security system was installed in Symone's home, a few more things were added that she wasn't aware of like a few hidden cameras that were strategically placed in her common areas. Charmaine was rolling on the floor, laughing her ass off at what she had just witnessed. It was so great to know that she wasn't the only one who was crazy.

# Good Morning Turkey

Fried turkey. Homemade cornbread stuffing. Collard greens. Even the distinct smell of chitterlings wafted in the air at Keyon's house. It was Thanksgiving Day, finally. His mother Carolyn and father Keith, along with Jynx's parents were in the kitchen getting busy on the food. Each year, the Steele family hosted the big meal at a different relative's house. This year was Keyon's turn. He didn't know what was going down, but he felt as if something good was going to happen today. He was thankful for family.

• • • • • • • • • • • • • • • • •

Jynx was uber excited. Today, before all of her family and close friends, she and Jonathan would announce their engagement. It had been hard keeping it secret but Jonathan wanted her entire family to be a part of the excitement. He was always thinking of her, she mused, sitting on the edge of her bed. She fingered the outline of the silk blouse that lay next to her on the bed that he had purchased for her at Bloomingdale's the other day. He had an uncanny eye for fashion, more than any man she'd ever known. He could style her better than June Ambrose. Picking up the shirt and hugging it to her body, she got up and danced around the room. Yes, she was extremely happy this Thanksgiving morning. She was thankful for reciprocated love.

• • • • • • • • • • • • • • • • •

Roommates, Cha-Cha and Devine were in the mirror primping. They would be spending Thanksgiving with Keyon and his family. Today would be Cha-Cha's first time spending the holidays with another family besides her own, and the first Thanksgiving since her final gender reassignment surgery. No matter how much Devine tried to reassure her, she was still a bit apprehensive about joining strangers for such a personal holiday, especially knowing that Keyon's mom was a Christian. He was not in the mood to be judged by anyone. Devine said that Mrs. Steele was a gem and that he would be just as welcomed as any other member of the family. Both of them were thankful for acceptance.

● ● ● ● ● ● ● ● ● ● ● ● ● ● ● ● ●

Across town, Charmaine rested. She wasn't too big on holidays since her mom left. She planned to work on some New Year's Eve plans, but since she had company, she figured it would wait. She pulled her Cornish hens out of the oven and set her table. Her guest was getting comfortable downstairs, so she decided to pour them both a glass of orange juice. It was a peaceful start to her day. She was thankful that she wouldn't have to hurt anyone today.

● ● ● ● ● ● ● ● ● ● ● ● ● ● ● ● ●

Symone lay in bed staring at the ceiling. She knew Keyon's house was going to be packed with food, friends, family and fun. It would be nice to be a part of a big family again. Shymon was out of town and at the moment, she had no clue where Donnie was. She didn't come home last night or the day before. This was supposed to be their first Thanksgiving together. She was thankful that no one knew the truth about what was going on with her relationship.

● ● ● ● ● ● ● ● ● ● ● ● ● ● ● ● ●

Donnie woke up in a hotel between two beautiful women. They'd had a hell of a time last night. She knew she'd have some explaining to do to Symone, but it would be worth it. She was very thankful for good pussy.

• • • • • • • • • • • • • • • • •

Keyon's family was in the kitchen getting busy. They were laughing, cooking, dancing and singing. Everyone was in great spirits. Keyon's mom, Carolyn, realized at the last minute that she left a few pies, her special seasonings and a pot of greens.

"Honey, how did you go off and forget something so important?" her husband asked.

"Moving too fast, I guess. It's not a problem. I need to get a fresh blouse anyway. I'll be back in about twenty minutes," she said, kissing her husband goodbye. She was thankful for love that lasted.

• • • • • • • • • • • • • • • • •

Before the big Steele dinner, Keyon and the staff at Man of Steele Records was preparing dinner to feed the homeless. By the time Keyon and everyone arrived at the shelter things were well underway. For the end of November to be upon them, the weather was more indicative of a nice spring day. It was overcast, but the sun appeared to be fighting its way through the clouds, adding a touch of warmth to the day.

News crews and reporters were excited to cover the day's events. Shortly before the dinner was to be served, M.O.S Records and the city of Atlanta would be cutting the ribbon to unveil a new homeless facility. The building was able to seat twenty-five hundred people and held a large commercial kitchen with the latest appliances. There was also a resource center that would assist with job and housing searches. After the ribbon cutting ceremony and the dinner was served a reporter interviewed Keyon. There was a familiar face standing off to the side, looking at him menacingly. It was one of Big's henchmen. The man

169

discretely motioned for Keyon to follow him. They ended up at a black Lincoln Town Car with the license plate that read-BLUD-MNY where Big waited inside. Keyon got in.

"You have more money for me?"

"Not yet. I'm working on get-.."

"No Excuses. I don't think that you realize how serious I am about my gwap. Mouse, hit the switch," Big said. Keyon watched as the big man pulled a device out of his pocket and pressed a button. He was half expecting the shelter to blow up but breathed a sigh of relief when it didn't. The henchman turned his android phone around to show Keyon what happened. Keyon started screaming, but the other man punched him in the head to silence him.

"Please don't make a spectacle of yourself and draw attention to this car. I warned you but you didn't listen. I hate it had to come to this. I'm going on vacation. You have until January 5th to get me the four million you owe me or else more of what you just saw, will occur. Now get the fuck outta my car." Keyon got out of the car and frantically placed a call.

"Dad, is everyone still at my place?"

"Yeah, Son. We're all here. Well, except Mom. She had to get some things from the house."

"What! Mom is at home? Oh no!"

"What's wrong, Son?"

"I don't have time to explain now. Meet me at your house. NOW!" Keyon went to Judy and told her there was a family emergency and asked her to hold things together and then he left in a rush.

● ● ● ● ● ● ● ● ● ● ● ● ● ● ● ● ●

From the time the black car pulled up, to the goon getting out and his boss giving him orders, to the men getting in the car, she had seen it all. And she couldn't believe her eyes. It was him. The man in her dreams that she thought she would never see again. Of all the places where he would be it was here. Domynique thanked her lucky stars. Not that she was going to speak to him looking like the bum she was, but she was happy to just lay eyes on him. *He's even more handsome than I remember,* she fawned. What a small world. She sat right across the street from where he was and she was close enough to see the tears and worried look on his face. Whatever the person in the car said to him it was not good. Seeing him had made her day. She floated back to the area where they were serving dinner and got a plate.

•••••••••••••••••••

After they served almost two hundred and fifty people, Judy and Watson sat down under one of the large tents and rested.

"How's Keyon's case coming, Watt? Any leads?" Judy probed. Watson hadn't told her any of the case specifics but he shared his frustrations openly.

"Judy, I honestly believe that when people don't want to be found they know how far underground to go. This girl is like the Invisible Man. There's something I'm not seeing and I swear its right under my nose."

At that moment, a husky homeless man began to manhandle a small woman a bit too roughly and she was doing everything she could to avoid him. When she attempted to walk away, he held on to the cuff of her sleeve, pulling the dirty gray sweater off her shoulder.

"That's a damned pretty tattoo on your shoulder," he said almost menacingly. The lady didn't respond. He was about to say something else when Watson intervened.

"I don't think the lady wants to be bothered," he said to the man as the lady quickly adjusted her sweater. "Why don't you just keep it moving? Go get a tour of the shelter if you haven't already."

The man gave Watson the once over and decided against an altercation. "I done already had my tour. I'm 'bout ready for seconds anyway," he said to Watson. "Looks like that angel on your shoulder sent you some help," he said to the lady and walked away.

"Are you alright, Miss?" Watson asked when he turned around but realized he was talking to himself. She had disappeared. He told Judy about the incident when he rejoined her.

"Hmm, and you sure did notice a lot about this person considering you only saw her sixty seconds," Judy commented.

"That's my job," he answered smugly.

"What else did you notice about her and where else have you looked?" Judy asked.

"She wore this big ugly sweater and there was a tattoo…Son of a bitch! Judy, you're a genius!" Watson yelled excitedly. "I'll catch ya later."

"Uh, ok," she said, not knowing what she did. Judy stayed at the shelter another hour and then headed to Keyon's so that the family could start their holiday.

● ● ● ● ● ● ● ● ● ● ● ● ● ● ● ● ●

Symone sat in the middle of her bed crying. Donnie had just kicked her ass like she was a nigga on the street. When Donnie strolled in from wherever she had been, Symone immediately started in on her.

"Where the fuck you been, Donita? Your ass can't keep staying out all night, coming in when you feel like it. You owe me an explanation!" she yelled at the top of her voice.

"I don't owe you shit, 'Mone. You need to pump your muthafuckin' breaks before I knock the shit outta your bitch ass."

"Bitch? I ain't no bitch! And your punk ass ain't gon' do shit. I wish you would," she replied with a smirk on her face.

And Donnie granted her wish. She spun Symone around to face her and punched her directly in the mouth.

"That's for talking shit!" Donnie said, then slapped her hard. So hard that Symone flew into the sofa table, causing the lamp to come crashing to the floor, breaking into tiny pieces. While Symone was on the ground Donnie kicked her in the back and then sat on her legs. She punched her in the stomach, chest and sides repeatedly. Donnie was swinging like a windmill and after Donnie was winded, she stood up, kicked Symone again and spat on her.

"Now, get your bitch ass up and finish cooking my dinner. I invited people over to eat."

That was almost two hours ago. She finished cooking and while Donnie entertained in the living room, she sat alone in the bedroom listening to music, ashamed of the way she looked. Scratches marred her perfect complexion and an ugly bluish-purple bruise was beginning to darken under her right eye. There was a cut on her bottom lip and a shoe-print shaped bruise was on her right thigh. Her head ached and her body hurt to move but somehow she managed to make it to the bathroom, take two Advil, and get back into bed.

Donnie poked her head into the room and saw that Symone was listening to music with her headphones on. Knowing how shallow her lover could be, Donnie knew she wouldn't come out of the room in her condition, so she returned to her company.

"Hey, come here Juanita with yo' fine, thick ass," she said to one of her guests.

"Stone, you're awfully bold or stupid to be talking to me like that with your woman in the next room."

"Man, Symone don't care what I do. Shit, I run this. Now get your ass over here." The lady obliged and went to stand in front of Donnie who slid her hands under her skirt and palmed her ass cheeks like they were basketballs.

"Damn, this is a juicy booty. Y'all ain't had no shit like this before, have you?" Donnie asked her two other friends.

"Shee-it D, I bet your ass won't touch the punanny," her friend, Nick, challenged.

"Uh-oh! You don' challenged her," E said. "It's about to be on now."

Not one to resist a challenge, Donnie lifted Juanita's skirt and moved her thong to the side. She slid her index and middle fingers into the woman's hot box.

"Alright now Stone, don't start no shit, won't be no shit," Juanita informed her.

"Now you know I finish er' thang I start," Donnie said, before sliding the thong down over the standing girls' thighs and licked her nether lips. Donnie was just about to bury her face in her pussy when she had a second thought.

"Here, put these back on. We are gonna finish this at your place. Let's bounce," she told her friends. Everyone got up and headed to the door. Donnie stopped.

"Hold up, I need to tell my girl I'm rolling out with y'all. I can't have her worried."

"Bet. We'll meet you at the truck," Nick said, closing the door as she walked out. Donnie walked into the room and took the ear buds out of Symone's ears.

"Yo, I'ma roll with the crew a few hours. I'll be back." Then she leaned over and tongue kissed Symone, long and deep. "By the way, those stuffed peppers you made the other day got rave reviews. Er 'body thought they were the shit."

Even through the pain, Symone smiled.

# Thanks, For Giving...

Broken glass, wood and paper littered the street. Small fires smoldered in places that the water had yet to reach but the firefighters had aggressively fought the fire and it was all but out. Keyon had already been interviewed. The cops were now talking to his dad who had tears in his eyes. The bomb squad was searching for shrapnel. There were no words to be said. The Steele's had just suffered an indescribable loss. And it was all his fault.

"Hey, Earth to Keyon. Are you okay?" Cha-Cha asked.

"My bad. I was just thinking about everything that has happened. I'm numb."

Concerned about his friend, Cha-cha asked "What are you going to do?"

"Pay Big. My dad has offered me half the money. That leaves me 41 days to come up with the rest of the money. I've really fucked up, Cha. Business is going down and I don't know how I'm going to come up with the money."

"Don't worry. You'll get it."

"I hope so," he sighed. "My dad could hardly look at me. All I could see was hurt and disappointment in his eyes. They had threatened Symone before. I never imagined this though."

"Mama Carolyn will be just fine. She's blessed, Keyon. God got this."

Pain and frustration overtook Keyon and he started punching at the air. "I want to kill Big. I swear I do," he said thru angry tears. "If you come after me, I understand. But my

Mom? My motherfucking Mama! That's foul shit."

Cha-cha giggled. "I'on see shit funny, Miracha."

"I'm sorry, Keyon. I know this is serious. You just re-minded me of Cuba Gooding, Jr. in *Boyz in the Hood* when he was punching the air. Please forgive me. I'm not trying to make light of this situation. But lemme tell you this, you can't pick and choose when to trust God and now is not the time to start doubting him. Have faith, brother."

"I know you're right. Here comes my dad. What's up, Pops?"

"This is unreal, Son."

"Dad, I know and I'm so sorry. I never wanted any of this to happen. I know you're disappointed and I wa-.."

"Keyon, I don't think you can fathom what I'm feeling right now. That's my wife lying over there and it ain't a damned thing I can do to help her. She's my rib. The air that I breathe. Without her, there is no me."

Keyon couldn't reply. He just put his arms around his dad's neck and the two cried. Suddenly, a car pulled out and an older lady jumped out.

"Jesus, what done happened? Where is my, baby? Please take me to my child."

"She's over there, G-Steele. They're about to take her away," Keyon said to his grandmother.

"Baby boy, what happened?" Sorrowfully, Keyon told his grandmother the whole sordid tale. By the time he was fin-ished, she was crying, too. "Keyon, why didn't you come to your family for help, baby? Why did you have to go to crooks? Crooks, Keyon? I thought that I taught you better than this."

"Mama, the boy already feels guilty. Don't pile it on," Keyon's dad added.

"Hell, I'm just fucking with him. Shit happens. I wouldn't have borrowed money from the family either. Last thing you want is one of these mutherfucka's knowing your business. Family is sometimes dirtier than foes."

"That's true, G-Steele."

"Damn, I need a blunt. Cha-cha you got that loud?" Keyon's grandmother stated.

"Nah, it's been drought season this way."

"Mama, please stop all that cursing and the last thing you need to be talking about around the cops is drugs."

"Kiss my ass, Keith. You need to smoke something and loosen up. Now is the time to release some tension," she replied.

Leave it up to Keyon's grandmother to add comic relief to any situation. She was trying to find something to laugh about to mask the pain of her daughter being hurt. What monster would set explosives in someone's house on Thanksgiving Day? What kind of people had Keyon gotten hooked up with? Lillian Steele might be old, but she didn't get that way by being stupid.

The family saw that the paramedics were driving off so they jumped in their cars to follow them to the hospital. By the time they arrived every Steele that was at Keyon's house had arrived and bombarded the waiting room. Keyon was beside himself with guilt and worry, waiting to hear news about his mother. His dad paced the floor like an expectant father and his grandmother and great-grandmother prayed. They waited for what seemed like an eternity but only an hour had passed. When the emergency room door finally opened and the doctor walked through, everyone who was sitting stood. It became so quiet one could hear a pin drop.

However, the doctor did not stop in the waiting room to update the family. Instead he kept moving until he met the incoming ambulance to assist with the trauma victim that was coming in. All eyes were on him and no one noticed when the door opened again. Cha-cha was the first to see the person standing there.

"Mama Carolyn, you're okay. Praise God!" Everyone bum rushed her.

"Give her some air everybody, damn," Keyon's grandmother said.

"Mama, please stop cussing," Keyon's dad replied.

"Honey, I'm so glad that you are okay. What did the doctor

say?"

"They gave me a clean bill of health and told me I was free to go but not to get too excited," Carolyn informed.

"Won't God do it? He answered our prayers."

Keyon looked like he wanted to cry. "Mama, I'm so sorry. Can you please forgive me?"

"Son, there's nothing to forgive. I love you. Now, someone please tell me that you turned off the food at Keyon's or else we are going to have two houses up in smoke today," Carolyn responded.

Everyone nodded yes and laughed.

Suddenly, Keyon's phone vibrated in his pocket. *I knew mom was there. Next time u won't b so lucky. Consider this my Christmas gift 2 U. C-ya in January.* Disgusted and frustrated, he threw his phone into the wall. Some of his family members who didn't know what was going on assumed he did that because of what had just happened to his parent's home.

"Was that from him, Son?" his dad asked.

"Yeah. Pops, I'm sick of this shit."

"I know. We'll work it out. You have a little time. We'll work it out."

"I'm sorry about the house, dad. Whatever I have to do to make it right, I will."

"Don't worry about that. Your mother is what was important."

"I know, but we have so many memories there. All the pictures and mementos. Those things can't be replaced." Keyon felt horrible.

"Everything that's important to us had been moved to your great grandmother's house last year. All of our important documents are in a safe deposit box and anything else of value is in fireproof safe. We can retrieve it after the investigation is over."

"Wow, Dad. That's awesome. A huge relief."

"Yeah, that's your mother's doing."

"Let's get out of this hospital. It's almost six o'clock. We

178

can still get home and get our grub on," Carolyn suggested.

"Alright, Mama," Keyon said.

After the Steele's left the hospital, it looked empty. Amidst the tears and praises that went up, the Steele's realized that they had more to be thankful for than the average family. Especially Keyon. It had been some day. Big got his attention and he didn't care if he had to sell Man of Steele Records to get the money. He would never put himself in that type of situation again. He was deep in thought when Jynx came over to him.

"Hey fam, Watson and Judy both say they've been trying to get in touch with you. I told them your phone was broken. They're on their way. Watson said he has something for you. They know about the house and sent their blessings as well."

"Cool. I'm going to go to my room for a minute. I really need to be alone for a while."

"Understandable. I'll come get you when they get here."

An hour later, Watson and Judy stood in the foyer with a guest. Cha-cha ran over to the people and gasped.

"Motherfucker! Lemme go get Keyon." She ran up the stairs three at a time until she reached the top.

"Keyon, get your ass downstairs right now, nigga! Watson and Judy are here. And you're not gonna believe who else."

"A'ight. Let me wash my face!" Keyon yelled.

Moments later, he walked down the stairs and stopped on the last step. He wiped his eyes and shook his head to make sure he was seeing properly. Slowly, he came off the last step and walked towards Watson. He was so entranced with the person standing next to Watson that he didn't realize the music was no longer playing in the house and that all of his family was watching his every move.

Keyon was mesmerized by the beautiful woman. Without taking his eyes off her face, he picked up her small 5'2 inch frame and kissed her deeply on the mouth, happy that she kissed him back. His tongue explored her peppermint tasting mouth and wrestled with hers. He nibbled her lips and kissed her neck, behind her ear and back to her mouth. The kiss was so intense it took his mother to break them up because he forgot that they were not alone.

"Keyon, it's kids here. This is a family friendly event," his mother said.

He slowly placed her back on the floor, eyes still on her. "Is it really you?" Keyon asked.

"Yes."

"Your voice is as soft and beautiful as you are."

Watson cleared his voice. "Domynique Segar this is Keyon Steele."

"It's my pleasure to finally meet you. I've dreamt about you."

She blushed. "So have I. I'm very sorry. I never meant to hurt you."

"We'll talk about that later. Right now, let me introduce you to my parent's and the rest of the family. The introductions went quickly and everyone seemed to genuinely like Domynique. One of Keyon's teenaged cousins asked Domynique if anyone had ever told her that she looked like Lauren London's twin. The video vixen simply smiled and said no.

"Is that your real hair?" Shymon asked.

Domynique giggled. "Yes."

"Damn! I know chicks that would kill to have hair like that. Real or fake." he commented.

"I know. Me too," Jynx agreed.

The family talked about weaves, fake eye lashes and G-Steele's weed addiction a while and then Jonathan, Jynx's man, tapped his glass with a spoon to silence the room.

"Hey everyone. When I woke up this morning, I promise I had no clue that my day would be as eventful as it has been today. One thing I learned is that things can change in a blink of an eye and life is too valuable to waste. With that being said, I want all of you to know that I asked Dr. Jacobi for his daughter's hand in marriage and he gave his permission and Jynx said yes! She's gonna be my wife, y'all!"

The family offered their congratulations and well wishes

to the happy couple and made their way back for second and third helpings. Carolyn felt the hairs stand up on the back of her neck and went to the kitchen. Her husband followed.

"Are you okay, my love? I know today hasn't been easy."

"I'm fine. But I'm feeling like I was at the house. Oh Keith, it was awful. I'd just come from the cellar getting my seasonings when all of the hairs on my body stood up. I grabbed everything I went home for and high-tailed it out of the house. I was barely three houses away when ours exploded. All I could think about was you and Keyon."

"It's over now, baby. We're gonna be okay. You don't think it's another bomb, do you?"

"No. I just feel like I'm being watched. Come outside on the front porch with me for a sec."

• • • • • • • • • • • • • • • • • •

Symone sat in her car with her binoculars watching her friends and the people she used to call family eat, drink and be merry. Lucky, Jynx's eighteen-year-old sister, stood in front of the plate glass window with a kool-aid smile on her face, talking to someone whose face was blocked by a plant.

"Come on; move a little to the right so I can see you," Symone said, talking to herself. As if she heard her, Lucky reached out and pulled the person close to her.

"Da fuck? How you gon' spend the holiday with a nigga who cheated on your sister instead of her? My brother is a moth-erfuckin' traitor and I'm gonna get his ass told today! He can either be my brother or Keyon's homie, but he can't be both." Symone was livid as she prepared to get out of the car. She had piled on a ton of makeup before she left the house but still donned her sunglasses. She fidgeted under her seat for her hair-brush and brushed her matted weave so she would be decent when she got to the door.

Keyon's parents made it to the edge of the driveway just as Symone did.

"Hey Mr. and Mrs. Steele," she said politely.

"Hello," they said in unison.

"Umm, I was just gonna go in and say hey to everyone and speak at my brother."

"Keith, give us a minute, will ya'?" When he saw his wife's eyes slit and her fist ball up at her side, like Ms. Sophia in *The Color Purple*, he knew it was time to go. Without saying goodbye, he turned on his heels and walked quickly into the house.

"Symone, why are you really here?"

"I told you. I wanted to say hey to everyone and hol…"

"Please don't insult my intelligence by lying to me. The truth is you wanted to see who was at my son's house. I'm sure you got angry when you saw your brother's car here. You want him to be mad at my son just because you are."

Symone tried to deny it. "Shymon is a grown man. He can do what he wants to do."

"Baby, listen to me," Carolyn said, removing Symone's glasses slowly from her eyes. "You deserve better. I understand you're with some woman now."

"Don't judge me, Ms. Carolyn."

"I'm not judging you, Symone. It's your life. But the abuse only gets worse from here. I know you may want to come in, but we've had enough drama today. Does your partner know you're here?"

"I can do whatever I want to do."

"That purple bruise under your eye tells me differently."

"I need to talk to Keyon," she said, trying to walk around the woman but was blocked.

"Keyon has a special guest Symone. I don't think that's a good idea."

"Lauren London?"

"Excuse me?"

"Is Lauren London Keyon's special guest?" she said, pointing to the beautiful woman on the porch. Carolyn turned to see who she was talking about.

"That's Domynique, not Lauren London but yes, she is Keyon's guest. If you wanna talk to Shymon or Keyon call and ask them to come out. But do you really want your brother to see you disheveled like this? And if I can see your black eye and bruises, don't you think he will, too?"

Symone touched her face, embarrassed. She was becoming unwrapped and it was visible to everyone.

"Um, just tell everybody Happy Thanksgiving. I'll call my brother later." Symone walked off before Carolyn said anything else. If she didn't know it before, she knew it now. She was all alone. The fun and merriment continued in Buckhead, even though a light rain shower began to come down. But on the other side of town, with no rain in sight, a very deadly storm brewed.

# Big Girls Don't Cry..

A few days after Thanksgiving, Symone figured it was time for her to get even. Donnie was making her look like a fool in the streets and everyone knew about it. She could only imagine how people must be talking about her behind her back, especially her co-workers. It was out in the open that she and Keyon were no longer together and that she'd gotten with a woman. Her relationship was now swimming in the rumor mill. Earlier, while Symone was in the bathroom, masturbating of all things, one of her so-called friends walked into the ladies room and began talking about her.

"I can't believe she left fine ass Keyon for a damned, broke ass dyke. No job. Living off of her. Using her credit cards at leisure. Ol' girl is a trick."

"Me either, girl. I don't want a nothing ass nigga so why in the hell would I want a nothing ass bitch?" Symone recognized that voice coming from her friend and producer, Mona Drew.

"Exactly. That's that dumb shit I be talking about. Like Miche'le leaving Dre for fat ass, Suge."

"Some women have it so good and don't even realize it. Keyon is a good man."

"Didn't he cheat on her? I don't know if I could stay no matter now rich or fine he is."

Symone gave the speaker a high five in the stall.

"That's what she claims but I've met him and let me tell you, if ever a man loved a woman, he loved her. But if being with a woman is what she wants, then more power to her."

"I feel you. My homegirl is a lez and she knows Symone's chick. Word on the street is that she is a straight ho. Have dildo, will travel."

"Damn! This bitch be driving around all day in her Range Rover, smoking weed, and when she comes to pick Symone up, the gas tank be on E. I heard them arguing about it the other day."

"Hell naw, Mona. But her loss is my gain. I've been eyeing Keyon since I was at his anniversary bash. Now that he's single, he's free to mingle."

"What? Your ass got a man."

"Yep, a woman, too. But I need a new sponsor."

That was the last thing Symone heard before they walked out of the door. While she was masturbating to get off, Donnie was out licking and sticking other bitches. What she'd just heard wasn't anything new. Symone knew her girlfriend was unfaithful. But she had something for her and the bitches she fucked.

Symone began to replay the conversation she overheard in her head. The unknown chick seemed to know an awful lot about what her and Donnie had going on. Too much. Like she knew Donnie better than she let on. When Symone saw Mona later, anger rose like bile in her throat and it was hard for her to speak to her new frenemy.

"Shake that shit off, Symone. Big girls don't cry. We get even."

It took a lot for her to pretend like she was still cool with Mona, but if she was going to find out who the other chick was; she had to play the game.

"Hey Mona, girl. What's popping? You ready to take this show to the next level?"

"Hey Bestie, you already know. They don't call me Super Producer for nothing."

"I know, right. Hey, earlier, I saw you walk into the ladies room, talking to someone. Was that Alicia from Accounting?"

"Alicia? No, that was Juanita from Marketing. She's good people. The three of us should get together and hang out sometimes. You'd like her. I think you two have a lot in common."

*Too much in common if you ask me*, Symone thought. "You know I'm down." Symone smiled plastically. "Just let me know when and where."

For the next two hours, Symone was only focused on putting on the best show to date. Since hooking up with Donnie, she lost sight of what was really important, and that was her career. But today, she brought her A game. After the show, Mona suggested that the three of them hit happy hour. Juanita was going to be late. Mona said she had some loose ends to tie up at work. Reluctantly, Symone agreed, but was glad that she did after she had her first drink.

"So, how long have you been hanging out with Juanita?" Symone asked, taking a sip of her drink.

"Just since the company picnic in June. Feels like I've known her all my life. We just clicked, I guess," Mona replied.

Before Symone said anything else, Juanita walked up looking like a million dollars in her black Ralph Lauren cardigan fitted sweater and low rise capri's. She donned a pair of signature Ralph Lauren shades that made her look like a supermodel.

"Hey boo," she said to Mona and kissed her on both cheeks. "Sorry I'm late. Russell has a critical presentation tomorrow and I had to help him finish."

"Business before pleasure. Lemme introduce you to my bestie, Symone. Symone, Juanita." The women exchanged greetings.

"I'm a huge fan of your show. You knocked it out of the park today!"

"Thank you. I'm glad you liked it," Symone replied.

The three ladies took their drinks to a booth in the corner and sat down to talk. Symone was still playing a game with the ladies, but she was genuinely enjoying being out of the house for a change.

"What you over there skinning and grinning about?" Mona asked Symone.

"Not much. Just thinking about the show and the direction I want my career to go."

"Do you have plans to take it to television? Maybe be like Wendy? She has a great show," Juanita questioned.

"Maybe." Symone shrugged. "But I'm not going to rush anything. In due time."

"While you're on your grind, are you going to put love on the back burner like most career women today?" Juanita questioned.

"Look at you all in her business," Mona said lightly.

"I'd like to think of myself as a Renaissance woman, Juanita. I can do both. I may even have kids one day," Symone returned.

"Kids? But aren't you a les... I'm so sorry. Please forgive me. I'm not judging you. I like chicks sometimes, too," Juanita said.

Symone pretended to look shocked at her revelation. "It's cool. I'm still trying to figure out if I'm a true lesbian or not. I mean, it is true that I have a girlfriend right now, but I don't know if I like *all* women. I still love men."

"She must be something special to leave your ex for," Juanita pressed.

Mona sat quietly with raised eyebrows, interested in Symone's answers.

"Keyon and I just didn't work out, but I didn't leave him for her. Me and my girl were friends first but when I was ready for more, she was just what I needed. I'm enjoying where I am right now so I don't really know what the future holds."

"None of us do," Mona finally spoke.

"That's true. I have a, uh, friend who's a stud. Has lots of admirers. Tons of 'em. Do you date a fem or a stud?" Juanita inquired.

"A stud. We have a great relationship," Symone lied. "I

188

have never been treated the way she treats me." At least that part was true.

"Is that right? Um, does your license plate on your truck say 'SYMONSZ' on it?" Juanita asked.

"Yeah, why?" Symone said, giving Juanita the side eye.

"I thought that was your truck," she said, snapping her fingers. "I was in your condo community on Thanksgiving, visiting my, friend. She made me feel, very uh, welcome in her new place."

Symone smiled. "That's what friends are for."

"Yeah. I was making my Thanksgiving rounds. But instead of me eating, I chose to get eaten," Juanita replied with a smirk.

"What?" Mona almost spit out her drink.

"Girl, my friend asked me to come over so that she could taste me. You know I let her."

"You didn't?" Mona asked.

"Like hell," Juanita continued, "From the moment we spoke on the phone I knew what it was. When she opened the door and showed me to that soft, Cerulean colored, Italian leather sofa, I was already wet. I stood in front of her and she slid her fingers inside of me and eased my nectar down. I only had on a thong so it gave her easy access."

"Cerulean? That's Symone's favorite color. I don't know why you bougie bitches don't just say blue," Mona said, laughing.

"On Thanksgiving?" Symone asked quietly, turning a deep shade of red.

They didn't break the mold when they made her sofa, but how many people in her condo community had that same sofa? And how many studs lived there? Was this bitch telling her on the sly that she'd fucked Donnie in *her* house? While she was in the next room? Bile burned her esophagus as Juanita finished her story.

"Yes, girl. On Thanksgiving. Then we took it to my house to finish the job." Juanita winked.

"Juanita your ass is wild," Mona replied.

Symone sat speechless, feeling ill and fighting back tears. "If she has as many admirers as you say she does, surely she has to be spoken for."

"What does that have to do with me? If she doesn't care about her woman, why should I?" Juanita finished, looking Symone directly in the eyes. "She's the one who made the commitment, not me. I can have her whenever I want to. No strings attached. I'm winning!"

Juanita smiled deviously at Symone. Silently challenging her as if she wanted Symone to confront her. At that moment, Symone hated Juanita with everything she had within her and vowed to get even. She couldn't wait for them to leave. At a quarter to six, the trio said their goodbyes.

"I had so much fun," Mona announced.

Symone didn't reply, she only nodded her head in response.

Juanita yawned. "I need to get some sleep. I stayed overtime working on that one hundred and fifty page report due tomorrow morning. I'm burned out!"

"A hundred and fifty pages?" Mona shouted.

"Yes, girl." Juanita shook her head. "My whole career depends on it. See y'all tomorrow!" She winked at Symone and switched away.

After she left the cantina, Symone rushed back to the radio station and headed straight for Juanita's cubicle. Symone, threw open her desk drawer and poured a steaming cup of coffee on her report, ruining it. Then she unplugged her computer and poured nail polish remover inside the monitor and computer tower so she couldn't recover the document if she tried.

Since Juanita wanted to fuck with Donnie, Symone was going to fuck with her. But she was preparing something way more sinister for her lying lesbian lover that would put an end to her unfaithful ways once and for all.

# Happy Black Friday...

Keyon dreamt that he was a fly caught in a spider's web. No matter which way he moved, he was trapped and could not get out. He was the fly, Big was the spider. With every move he made it was as if more thread was being wrapped around him. He could not move; he could not breathe. The spider was about to consume him. Just before the spider's fangs penetrated his flesh; he was released from the web and propelled into a dark tunnel. He wandered aimlessly in the dark, groping the sides of the walls, feeling his way along. A light appeared at the end of the tunnel.

"You saved me, baby. Now, I'm going to save you," the angelic voice said. "I love you, baby. Come to me."

"I love you, too."

He ran towards the voice in the light. Happy that he was being rescued. A figure appeared in the light. It was Domynique. She was his savior. She stretched her arms out to welcome him. He was so close to her he could see the diamonds sparkle in her eyes. He was almost there. But then a shadow appeared behind the light. The spider was back. Keyon screamed but no sound came out.

"Move!" he screamed in his mind, but she couldn't hear him.

The spider crept closer to her. Keyon reached for her but the spider had spun a web around her and pulled her away from him. Large fangs dripped with venom over Domynique. Hot tears ran down Keyon's face. Domynique still smiled. She didn't realize she was in danger. Keyon got to her just as the spider's fang bit down. Slowly she slid out of the spiders grasp to the ground and he watched as the light diminished, propelling him into darkness once again.

"No!" he screamed.

"Baby! Baby, wake up. You're having a bad dream," Domynique said.

Keyon opened his eyes to see Domynique, then sat up and grabbed her, holding onto her tightly. "I can't breathe," he heaved. "I'm sorry. I'm so sorry. I thought I had lost you. I was so scared."

"It was only a dream. I'm not going anywhere. I'm here as long as you want me to be."

"It seemed so real. I know we just met and you just came into my life, but I don't want to lose you. I would kill myself if something happened to you."

"Keyon, it was only a dream."

"Domynique, I'm not perfect. I fucked up in my last relationship because I wanted to be a strong man and I felt like I was doing that by keeping certain things from my ex-fiancé, but I was wrong. There's something I need to tell you."

Keyon exhaled and for the next hour he told Domynique everything regarding his dealing with Big and how his debt was wreaking havoc in his life and lives of those he loved. He told her about all of the threats and how Big blew up his parent's home. He didn't want any secrets and wanted to start off with a clean, honest slate. Domynique did too, but she didn't tell him that she'd seen him yesterday. She knew what Big looked like and the henchmen that came after Keyon. It wasn't her intention to keep that from him, but he was already worried about her and she didn't want to add anything more to it.

"I have a little over a month to get the rest of the money and I know I will. But I really don't know what's going to happen after this. Sometimes things like this are never over."

"Thank you for telling me this. Whatever I can do to help you, I will. You saved me baby and I will help save you. Why are you looking at me like that?"

"In my dream, you said something similar to that."

"That's the only thing about your dream that's true."

Keyon looked into her eyes and pulled her face close to his. His lips grazed hers gently at first. Then he used his tongue to part her lips and explore her mouth. As the kiss deepened, her need for him intensified. She leaned back into the pillows and Keyon covered her body with his. He kissed her lips, her neck and her collar bone, traveling down to her ample bosom. The slip she had on slid easily off her shoulder, exposing her firm C-cup breasts. The heat from his mouth made her nipple harden and the suckling created an unfamiliar ache between her thighs.

She moaned in his mouth as his fingers traveled up her thigh and rested in the center of her love. His fingers found solace in her cream and he used her natural lubricant to stimulate her further. Her legs moved restlessly beneath him so he took that as a hint and used his knee to part them and get them out of his way. Somehow, the panties she wore ended up off and Keyon's mouth was now where his fingers used to be. Domynique had never experienced anything like this before. Tiny pulses of electricity eased from her toes and traveled up her legs. She felt like she was going to float away so she used Keyon's strong, muscular shoulders as an anchor.

Keyon could feel her pleasure and knew that she was about to cum. He wanted her to. The last time he had tasted her nectar he was too zonked to remember anything. This time he was going to savor every inch of her. Even early in the morning, her breath was minty so he was very curious to see what the rest of her tasted like. Domynique's legs began to shake and her breathing pattern changed. He was fucking her pussy with his tongue and she was crying in pleasure. He inserted two fingers into her tight, wet box and sucked her clit. Her legs tensed up and the dam was just about to break when someone knocked hard on his bedroom door.

"Fuck! Who is it?" he yelled.

"Your mother. Breakfast is ready. You and Domynique

193

come on down."

"Ugh. I have got to buy my parents a new house. I can see that this living arrangement is not going to work."

Domynique laughed. "It's okay. Your entire family is still here. They're still enjoying the holiday."

"Babe, I'm sorry. I wasn't trying to rush you. I really wanna get to know you before we make love. I just got carried away with that kiss."

"Keyon, you don't have to apologize. I wanted it as much as you."

"Can I ask you something serious?"

She knew this was coming. "Yes. Anything."

"You were a virgin when you made that tape."

"Yeah."

"Why would you want your first time to be with a total stranger? Did Big threaten you?"

"When I first saw you, I *wanted* to be with you. You were so handsome and you seemed to want me to. I guess it was the drugs. I wasn't working with Big though." Domynique didn't even want to begin telling Keyon who she was really working with. But at some point she'd tell him the truth.

"Then who…?" Suddenly, another knock came to the door. It was Cha-cha.

"Keyon, your mama said get your ass down here right now or else."

"Let's go. My family ain't gon' give us any privacy."

"Okay."

Before they went downstairs, Keyon's business cell phone vibrated. It was Symone texting him back.

*"Can we meet 2moro?"*

*"Yes. Hz 2 b early tho."*

*"Ok. Can u come 2 my job around 8am?"*

*"Yep. Thx Symone. I appreciate ur help."*

*"No worries. I got ur back."*

Keyon held his phone out. He wanted to be honest with Domynique. "That was Symone. She's loaning me some money to pay this debt. Is that okay?"

"Anyone willing to help you is alright with me. What happened between you two though?"

"We have plenty of time to talk about that," he told her, kissing her on the cheek then putting his phone back in his pocket.

"Yep. The rest of our lives."

"I like the way that sounds."

Keyon's phone vibrated again. This time what he saw sent him over the top. Venom filled his veins. It was a picture text from Big. Keyon had to refocus his eyes to make sure he was seeing correctly. Big had removed Keyon's business moniker 'Man of Steele Records' and replaced it with 'Big Steele Records.'

The text read:

*Nice pic, huh? Which would u rather lose? Ur life or ur business? U know how much I like choices so I'll let u decide.*

*Big*

A lump formed in Keyon's throat. At the moment he knew the only way to finally get rid of Big was to find a way to pay him, or resort to something more deadly.

# The Beginning Of The End...

Charmaine watched her monitors closely focusing her attention on monitors set up at Symone's house. She turned the volume up so that she could hear what Donnie was lying about now.

"Baby, I know things have been rocky between us, but I promise that you're the only woman I want and need," Donnie explained.

*I heard that shit before*, Charmaine thought.

"Then why cheat on me? I thought you were different. But now I see that being with a woman ain't no different than being with a man. You're just like Keyon."

"Don't! Ever! Compare to me that nigga!" Donnie said firmly before softening her demeanor again. She was trying to make amends with Symone, not scare her. If Symone left her, she'd be up shit creek.

"Listen, babe. I'm not like that cat. I love you. I've made some mistakes. Let these bitches get in my head when I know I got you here at home waiting for me. I'm not going to do anything to jeopardize that again. You mean too much to me. I see something very special in you."

*Yeah, dollar signs,* Charmaine thought.

Symone just sat there without speaking. She knew that Donnie loved her and the feeling was mutual but the two of them would have to make drastic changes in order to restore their relationship.

"Babe, you still love me?" Donnie asked seductively.

"You know I do."

"Well, come over here and show me," she said, beckoning for Symone to come over to her.

Pushing her against the wall gently, Donnie whispered, "I love you," just before their lips met. Her kiss was so sweet, her lips were always so soft as she gingerly sucked and nibbled on Symone's lips. Relaxing her mind, Symone concentrated on what Donnie was doing to her.

"God you smell good," Donnie said breathlessly as her lips moved expertly over Symone's jaw and down her neck, making her dizzy.

"Good enough to eat?" Symone asked as Donnie continued her path over Symone's shoulders. Her brain started feeling foggy as Donnie's kisses became more urgent.

She heard Donnie whisper, "I need you," pulling her nipple into her hot mouth.

It was all Symone needed to hear and feel to make her knees go weak. Donnie's tongue continued to work over her nipples, urgently alternating between the twin peaks. Even though she was at odds with her lover, Symone loved how Donnie made her feel. No words had to pass between them, Symone could feel Donnie's need for her and it matched her own.

Donnie's hands slid over Symone's thighs, now slick with her juices, lifting her gown slightly as she started to rub circles around her clit. She pressed her body against Symone's and whispered directly in her ear, "Cummmm for me, babyyyy," making Symone pull her close and moan into Donnie's mouth when she kissed her.

High pitched noises came from Symone's throat as she started to gasp and cum on Donnie's hand, still holding her close.

"Mmmmm, yeah that's it," Donnie whispered, kissing her cheek and smiling.

She kissed Symone's cheek and got on her knees in front of her. Donnie licked Symone's inner thighs giving her butterflies in her stomach. Symone lifted her leg slightly as Donnie moved her thong over and dove quickly into Symone's waiting wet pussy.

"Ooohhhh Goddddd," Symone moaned as her head rolled back.

Her breath came in quick gasps. Her head was spinning as she tried to steady herself. Donnie slid her other hand's fingers between Symone's lips and up into her entrance curling it towards her and rubbing gently with a perfect rhythm.

Feeling her orgasm start to build again Symone moaned, "Ohhh, yeah, I'm sooo close mmmm," making Donnie moan into her clit as she continued to suck and move her tongue quickly over it.

It was just what Symone needed to send her over the edge. Donnie could feel Symone's muscles clenching as she rocked on her face grinding into her tongue licking out the last remnants of a powerful orgasm. She smiled as she took one last lick and pulled her finger out of Symone, licking her sweet juices from it.

Standing up and kissing Symone, Donnie smiled and said, "Do you mind fixing me a sandwich? Nick is on her way over and we're going out for a while."

Charmaine was rolling on the attic floor laughing her ass off. That was typical Donnie. Reel you in and then leave you dangling on the hook. Symone looked like she wanted kill Donnie.

"I been there before too, girl," Charmaine said to the monitor.

But she didn't have sympathy for Symone. What did the home wrecking bitch expect? If Donnie cheated on Charmaine with Symone then she would cheat on Symone with someone else.

She watched as Symone fixed Donnie a turkey and Swiss cheese croissant. "What the hell is that?" Charmaine asked the monitor, cocking her head and moving her face in closer to the screen. "And people say I'm crazy. This bitch right here is the one."

In her kitchen, Symone pulled out a zip lock bag that was half full of the nastiest, slimiest maggots she could find. She squished the nasty larva before adding icing to the bag. Then she clipped the corner and squeezed the mixture on a cupcake that was baked with pecans, dead roaches, crickets and cat piss. Once Donnie was finished dressing, fake dick included, she went to the kitchen and picked up her sandwich.

"This shit right here is the business." She pointed at the croissant. "Awe, shit, baby girl done outdid herself and made me a cupcake."

"Don't do it, D. I can never kiss you after this if you do," Charmaine said laughingly at the screen.

But it was too late. Donnie's greedy ass downed the cupcake in two bites and licked her lips afterwards. Charmaine shook her head. Symone was a sneaky bitch and although she was not as cunning and crafty as Charmaine was, Char knew that she would have to keep a very close eye on her.

Charmaine turned her attention to monitor six, which was in the basement of her own house. She had a guest and wanted to make sure that she was okay then she returned her attention to Donnie and Symone. Symone was standing in the kitchen, drinking a glass of wine, giving Donnie the side eye.

"Come on, babe. Don't be like that," Donnie said. "Me and the Nick just making a quick run."

"I don't understand why you always have to leave after we make love."

"Shit just be coming up at the wrong time. But I promise I'm coming right back. Bring that pretty ass over here and lemme lick that good ass pussy again. I'm still hungry."

The couple undressed again but never made it to the bedroom. Charmaine watched them go at it like rabbits in heat, waiting patiently, eating popcorn. Donnie was licking vigorously. Symone was getting ready to come.

"Oh, yes, baby I'm almost there. Damn, baby. I love the way you love me." Symone's legs wrapped around Donnie's head as the orgasm began to overtake her. "I love you, Donita. I really want this to work between us."

"I know, babe and I love you, too. Tell you what, how about I stay in with you tonight instead of going out with Nick. We can make some popcorn and watch movies."

"Really, babe? I'd love that. And tomorrow when I come from the station, let's hop a plane and go some place warm. Anywhere you wanna go."

"Symone, on some real nigga shit, I ain't never loved no one the way that I love you and I put that on my brother."

Charmaine fumed at what she heard. She knew how much Donnie loved her brother and would never say anything like that if it wasn't true. She felt stupid for swimming an ocean for someone who wouldn't cross a puddle for her. Every woman that Donnie fucked with, Charmaine punished. The only reason she didn't do Symone like that was because Donnie told her not to mess with her and she didn't want to make Donnie angry. But it didn't matter anymore. Donnie had made her choice and Charmaine had made hers.

Around two a.m., Charmaine decided to do some mechanical work on a certain Range Rover. The wire cutters were not cutting the way she wanted them to. The front brake line on Symone's SUV was made of steel and a lot tougher for her to penetrate. She was able to make a hole in the line without cutting it completely and that satisfied her.

"Now to cut the emergency brake line and unhook the brake light and I'll be finished," Charmaine said out loud.

When her nemesis drove to work she was going to finally get what was coming to her. Charmaine was tired of dealing with that bitch and she was not going to tolerate her another day. Once Symone was out of the way, Donnie would be hers free and clear and they would get married just like Donnie promised.

Charmaine removed the navy blue coveralls after she got into her rented truck. It was late and Symone was going in around eight in the morning. She'd wait for Symone to come out in a few hours and follow her to make sure that her plans were carried out. The night Atlanta air had a bit of a chill so Charmaine grabbed her blanket out of the back seat and covered herself up. She listened to the internet radio on her phone and dozed off a little after two. A few hours later, an alarm clock buzzed waking Symone and Donnie.

"Good morning, babe," Donnie said, rolling over to kiss Symone.

"Good morning, sweety."

"Do you mind if I take you to work this morning? I need to take my car in to get some work done on it."

"I don't mind. Let me get up and get dressed and we can head out. I have a big day ahead," Symone replied. *I finally get to meet with Keyon. I'm going to tell him how much I love him and really miss him. Once I help him with this debt, he will see that I'm down for him.*

Symone hurriedly dressed and they left the condo. Even though Donnie was supposed to be dropping Symone off at work, she didn't want to drive right off. She was still sleepy and wanted to relax on the drive to her girl's job. Donnie got in and shut her door and that jarred Charmaine out of her sleep.

"Oh, shit. She's in the car," Charmaine said to herself, seeing Symone's leg lift into the sporty SUV and then shut her door. "And let the games begin." she said as Symone slowly backed out of her parking spot. Because she didn't cut the brake line all the way through, there was still going to be a little bit of pressure in the line to allow Symone to stop. But after a couple of minutes the fluid would all leak out and then stopping would be impossible. Especially since the emergency brake didn't work either.

Symone turned the volume up on the radio. Donnie turned it to the comedy channel on the satellite radio station she loved listening to and reclined her seat. When she pulled out of her complex the light was green and they didn't have to stop or slow down since she wasn't going very fast at first. Charmaine followed about three cars behind and waited for the chance to make her move. The SUV picked up speed as it made its way through the early morning traffic.

"Slow your ass down, Symone," Donnie said, unable to fall asleep.

"I'm not even doing 45mph. The speed limit is 50. Chill."

The light ahead was still green. It was smooth sailing for the two people. A garbage truck was coming down the street headed East as Symone drove south. She wasn't paying attention because she was too busy laughing at the comedian on the radio. Charmaine pulled up behind her and tapped her bumper.

"What the fuck!" Donnie yelled, sitting up.

"I don't know, baby. Some maniac is bumping us! Call 9-1-1!" Symone yelled.

Charmaine laughed hard as the truck in front of her began to bob and weave on the street. They were steadily approaching the light that had quickly turned from green to red. As if it was slow motion, Charmaine watched the scene play out before her. She broke hard so that she would not cross the intersection but Symone sailed through the red light at the same time that the garbage truck sailed through the green light. The sound of screeching tires from the truck and the loud sound of crushing metal woke the residents in the nearby homes.

Charmaine had no clue the truck was going to come, but she couldn't have planned it better if she tried. A huge smile spread across her face as she drove the truck back to the storage unit a few miles away and exchanged it for her taxi. Before leaving she made sure there was no damage on the cargo van and then she drove back to the accident site. The accident had caused traffic backups and it took her almost an hour to get back. Emergency and camera crews were on the scene and Charmaine watched them work. She got close enough so that she could hear and have a good view.

A reporter for Channel Three News was questioning an Atlanta Police Officer.

"Captain, we're getting different accounts of what happened here this morning. Can you shed some light on horrific accident?"

"Well, we received a call from 911 that a cargo van was aggressively bumping a 2009 Range Rover for reasons unknown, just driving aggressively behind the vehicle," the officer stated. "It happened just after four a.m. on the 85 South Service Road. The couple riding in that SUV called 911." The officer went back to the scene after giving his statement.

"We have the actual recording of the 911 call now." Moments later, the station aired the recording.

Dispatcher: Fulton County 911, what's your emergency?

Caller: Yes, we just exited 85 South on 17th Street, and a white van is following us. He's been following us and he keeps turning off his lights on and off. He just hit us! He just hit us!

Dispatcher: Ok, are you hurt?

Caller: No, but we're not going to stop. Do not stop, Symone. He keeps hitting us! He keeps hitting us!"

Charmaine heard the call. She knew the voice. If Symone was driving then that meant that Donnie was the passenger and the one placing the call.

Driver: Donnie, I'm going to hit somebody.

Caller: A truck is coming towards us. Jesus!

Dispatcher: Ma'am, ma'am. Calm down.

Seconds later, you could hear the crash on the 911 call and then the line went dead.

Charmaine shook in fear as the fire department began peeling back the metal in order to free the accident victims. There were two other cars involved in the accident that she didn't see because they were on the other side of the truck. A woman who was visibly pregnant was pulled from a small red Pontiac. Symone's truck was next. Paramedics rushed to the truck after the fire department got the doors opened. They pulled Symone out first. But her fears were confirmed when they pulled Donnie's body from the car.

"No! No! No!" Charmaine screamed out loud. *What have I done?*

TO BE CONTINUED...

# ABOUT THE PUBLISHER

Life Changing Books, more affectionately known as LCB, established in 2003, has become one of the most respected independent Trade Publishers amongst chain stores, vendors, authors and readers. LCB offers a variety of literature including, non-fiction, contemporary fiction, urban/street literature, and a host of other categories.

For more information visit us online at:
www.lifechangingbooks.net

Twitter: @lcbooks
Instagram: @lcbooks
Facebook: www.facebook.com/LCBooks

CHECK OUT THESE TITLES

BY: *Kendall Banks*

# CHECK OUT THESE LCB SEQUELS

# LCB BOOK TITLES

See More Titles At
www.lifechangingbooks.net

**Game Over**

*Over*

● My Love for Hip Hop ●

*Winter*

**RAMOS**

LOVE & HIP HOP REALITY STAR

# ORDER FORM

**MAIL TO:**
PO Box 423
Brandywine, MD 20613
301-362-6508

| Date: | Phone: |
|---|---|
| Email: | |

Ship to:
Address:
City & State:                    Zip:

*Make all money orders and cashiers checks payable to:* **Life Changing Books**

| Qty | ISBN | Title | Release Date | Price |
|---|---|---|---|---|
| | 0-9741394-2-4 | Bruised by Azarel | Jul-05 | $ 15.00 |
| | 0-9741394-7-5 | Bruised 2: The Ultimate Revenge by Azarel | Oct-06 | $ 15.00 |
| | 0-9741394-3-2 | Secrets of a Housewife by J. Tremble | Feb-06 | $ 15.00 |
| | 0-9741394-6-7 | The Millionaire Mistress by Tiphani | Nov-06 | $ 15.00 |
| | 1-934230-99-5 | More Secrets More Lies by J. Tremble | Feb-07 | $ 15.00 |
| | 1-934230-96-2 | A Private Affair by Mike Warren | May-07 | $ 15.00 |
| | 1-934230-96-0 | Flexin & Sexin Volume 1 | Jun-07 | $ 15.00 |
| | 1-934230-89-8 | Still a Mistress by Tiphani | Nov-07 | $ 15.00 |
| | 1-934230-91-X | Daddy's House by Azarel | Nov-07 | $ 15.00 |
| | 1-934230-88-X | Naughty Little Angel by J. Tremble | Feb-08 | $ 15.00 |
| | 1-934230820 | Rich Girls by Kendall Banks | Oct-08 | $ 15.00 |
| | 1-934230839 | Expensive Taste by Tiphani | Nov-08 | $ 15.00 |
| | 1-934230732 | Brooklyn Brothel by C. Stecko | Jan-09 | $ 15.00 |
| | 1-934230669 | Good Girl Gone bad by Danette Majette | Mar-09 | $ 15.00 |
| | 1-934230804 | From Hood to Hollywood by Sasha Raye | Mar-09 | $ 15.00 |
| | 1-934230707 | Sweet Swagger by Mike Warren | Jun-09 | $ 15.00 |
| | 1-934230677 | Carbon Copy by Azarel | Jul-09 | $ 15.00 |
| | 1-934230723 | Millionaire Mistress 3 by Tiphani | Nov-09 | $ 15.00 |
| | 1-934230715 | A Woman Scorned by Ericka Williams | Nov-09 | $ 15.00 |
| | 1-934230685 | My Man Her Son by J. Tremble | Feb-10 | $ 15.00 |
| | 1-924230731 | Love Heist by Jackie D. | Mar-10 | $ 15.00 |
| | 1-934230812 | Flexin & Sexin Volume 2 | Apr-10 | $ 15.00 |
| | 1-934230748 | The Dirty Divorce by Miss KP | May-10 | $ 15.00 |
| | 1-934230758 | Chedda Boyz by CJ Hudson | Jul-10 | $ 15.00 |
| | 1-934230766 | Snitch by VegasClarke | Oct-10 | $ 15.00 |
| | 1-934230693 | Money Maker by Tonya Ridley | Oct-10 | $ 15.00 |
| | 1-934230774 | The Dirty Divorce Part 2 by Miss KP | Nov-10 | $ 15.00 |
| | 1-934230170 | The Available Wife by Carla Pennington | Jan-11 | $ 15.00 |
| | 1-934230774 | One Night Stand by Kendall Banks | Feb-11 | $ 15.00 |
| | 1-934230278 | Bitter by Danette Majette | Feb-11 | $ 15.00 |
| | 1-934230299 | Married to a Balla by Jackie D. | May-11 | $ 15.00 |
| | 1-934230508 | The Dirty Divorce Part 3 by Miss KP | Jun-11 | $ 15.00 |
| | 1-934230316 | Next Door Nympho By CJ Hudson | Jun-11 | $ 15.00 |
| | 1-934230286 | Bedroom Gangsta by J. Tremble | Sep-11 | $ 15.00 |
| | 1-934230340 | Another One Night Stand by Kendall Banks | Oct-11 | $ 15.00 |
| | 1-934230359 | The Available Wife Part 2 by Carla Pennington | Nov-11 | $ 15.00 |
| | 1-934230332 | Wealthy & Wicked by Chris Renee | Jan-12 | $ 15.00 |
| | 1-934230375 | Life After a Balla by Jackie D. | Mar-12 | $ 15.00 |
| | 1-934230251 | V.I.P. by Azarel | Apr-12 | $ 15.00 |
| | 1-934230383 | Welfare Grind by Kendall Banks | May-12 | $ 15.00 |
| | 1-934230413 | Still Grindin' by Kendall Banks | Sep-12 | $ 15.00 |
| | 1-934230391 | Paparazzi by Miss KP | Oct-13 | $ 15.00 |
| | 1-93423043X | Cashin' Out by Jai Nicole | Nov-12 | $ 15.00 |
| | 1-934230634 | Welfare Grind Part 3 by Kendall Banks | Mar-13 | $15.00 |
| | 1-934230642 | Game Over by Winter Ramos | Apr-13 | $15.99 |
| | 1-934230618 | My Counterfeit Husband by Carla Pennington | Aug-14 | $ 15.00 |
| | 1-93423060X | Mistress Loose | Oct-13 | $ 15.00 |
| | 1-934230626 | Dirty Divorce Part 4 | Jan-14 | $ 15.00 |
| | | | **Total for Books** | $ |

\* Prison Orders- Please allow up to three (3) weeks for delivery.

Shipping Charges (add $4.95 for 1-4 books\*) $
Total Enclosed (add lines) $

Please Note: We are not held responsible for returned prison orders. Make sure the facility will receive books before ordering.

\*Shipping and Handling of 5-10 books is $6.95, please contact us if your order is more than 10 books. (301)362-6508

21101916R00120

Printed in Great Britain
by Amazon